D0316846

Peter Taylor was born in Sedgefield, County Durham, and has worked as both a teacher and prison lecturer.

A QUESTION OF LOYALTY

Investigating the murders of three men stirs up trouble for DI Alex Graham, causing him to relive a past tragedy. Working with his old lover, DS Best, Graham must delve deep into the men's military histories to find answers. Having witnessed one killing, and now hiding out in a safe house, Liz Hunt hears word of the other dead men — friends of her husband Danny, who has isolated himself on the North Yorkshire Moors. Is it disloyal to share her information with the detectives? DI Graham won't be resting until he can close this case — and with it, the door to his terrible past.

PETER TAYLOR

A QUESTION OF LOYALTY

Complete and Unabridged

ULVERSCROFT
Leicester

First published in Great Britain in 2014 by
Robert Hale Limited
London

First Large Print Edition
published 2015
by arrangement with
Robert Hale Limited
London

A catalogue record for this book is available
from the British Library.

ISBN 978–1–4448–2583–1

Published by
F. A. Thorpe (Publishing)
Anstey, Leicestershire

Set by Words & Graphics Ltd.
Anstey, Leicestershire
Printed and bound in Great Britain by
T. J. International Ltd., Padstow, Cornwall

As always, for my mother and father, but also remembering the lovely Elsie Watson of Alston, Cumbria, like her daughter, Vilma, a gracious lady.

The smartly dressed man stared across the table at his companion. It had been ten years since they'd met but Max Sinclair hadn't changed much, still had that air of cold, nasty calculation about him, as though a portion of his mind was constantly trying to work out an answer to a sum, never quite making it and leaving him resentful of the fact. Max had arranged this meet in a bar near King's Cross Station, such a different place from their first coming together an age ago in the sweltering heat of desert country.

'So,' Max said, slugging back his whisky like an old-time Hollywood cowboy. 'Business.'

The man hesitated. Once he broached the subject, there could be no going back. Could he be sure Max hadn't changed? Having come this far, he felt he had no other recourse than to chance his arm and anyway, men like Max didn't suddenly grow a conscience.

'I take it you're still involved in private security?' he said, cagily.

'What else? Keeps me in the manner to which I have become accustomed.' Max stared hard across the table. 'Unlike some, who grew up accustomed, eh?'

The man ignored the jibe. 'Remember when we met?'

Max frowned. 'As I recall, we had a few drinks together. I was contracted to an oil company at the time.' He sighed, the way another man might for a long-lost love. 'Nice little earner that was but I wasted most of it.'

The man managed a smile. 'A few drinks together would be understating it. We pushed the boat out a few times.'

Max picked up his glass, twirled it between his fingers, watched the liquid swirl. 'Me and my old friend Johnny Walker go back a long way. Sometimes he takes over the conversation, talks out of turn, most of it made up, of course.'

'Right now, I'm hoping something you told me wasn't a fabrication.'

Max's eyebrows rose. His eyes slid around the bar room, then returned to his companion, roamed over him like a forensic scientist examining a corpse for clues.

Finally, he said, 'You're a strange one. After all these years you seek me out, ask for a meet, then expect me to recall something I said when I was drunk in some flea-ridden bar a million miles from nowhere. Whatever it was, it must have been pretty momentous.'

The man inhaled deeply, like a diver on a

high board poised to take the plunge. One more step and he would be past the point of no return.

'You said, as a sideline to your main business, you hired out . . . killers.'

Max's body stiffened. His facial muscles pulled taut leaving cadaverous hollows beneath his cheekbones. Then a slow, mirthless smile brought his face back to life. His stare was as calculating as ever but there was a touch of wonderment too.

'Must have been very drunk to say a thing like that to a relative stranger.'

'You were and I never forgot it. It's what brought me here today.'

Max grunted. 'Even if I could remember, even if it was true and not some fantasy brought on by the drink, you think I would admit to it?'

The man hesitated, rubbed at a spot on his jacket. This was risky but he figured if Max was the man he thought he was, it would only be a miniscule risk. He was pretty sure he would be into things he shouldn't and, in the unlikely event he reported this conversation to the police, he would be drawing attention to himself. It was only a small gamble, really, and worth taking, all things considered.

'I'm working for somebody who needs to remove — how did he put it — 'two irritants'.

3

I thought if you were still working you might expedite such matters for him.'

Max sat back, leaned his head to the side, like a boxer weighing up an opponent. He was obviously wondering whether this was a put-up job, a kind of entrapment, perhaps, but he was also aware there could be no reason for that after the passing of so many years. Why would anyone wait so long to set him up?

'You just entered a minefield,' he said, his eyes like two black beads. 'So be very careful. If you're messing with me there are men who'll find you. Even if I'm dead, they'll find you. Professional etiquette amongst my kind. Mutual protection discourages chancers.'

'Understood. I've heard about that. You'll fix it, then . . . for my friend?'

'For twenty thousand a mark, I might. Your . . . friend . . . is he prepared to pay that?'

'He'd call it cheap at the price and I'm sure he'd make it fifty thousand all told for a prompt response.'

They stared at each other for a moment before Max spoke again.

'Okay, consider it a done deal.'

The man felt a measure of relief; everything seemed to have gone well. Reaching into the briefcase, he pulled out a folder, passed it across the table.

'Names, addresses, other information. It's all in there, plus a phone number for contacting me.'

Max took the folder from him, didn't open it and a silence descended. They were men from different worlds now and anything they said would seem trite after the business they'd just concluded. Into the silence, as though from another world, a more carefree world, came a burst of raucous laughter from a group of men at the bar. Max tucked the folder under his arm and rose.

'You pay in notes after they're dead,' Max said, smiling. 'I'll be in touch about how and when.'

Neither man extended his hand. They walked to the door side-by-side and then out into the bustle of a London night where they parted with a curt nod to each and set off in different directions. As he heaved a sigh of relief, in the dark alley across the street the man noticed a raddled prostitute approaching a car whose driver wound down the window and began negotiations. People would do anything for money, he reflected, and if you had it you might as well use it to ease your passage when trouble came to your door. He was glad, though, that his own sordid adventure was over and done, that soon he'd be out of the city and back to his life.

★ ★ ★

Liz Hunt lay on the bed in that seductive zone somewhere between sleep and wakefulness, not aware of where she was, just luxuriating in the numbing of her senses. Suddenly, she felt a blow on her shoulder and her eyes shot open. A momentary feeling of terror gave way to relief and not a little sorrow when she realized it was her husband's arm that had struck her. Beside her, Danny was thrashing about as though an evil spirit possessed him, his boyish face contorted, perspiration dampening both cheeks. Her heart aching for him, she reached out, pressed her palm gently against his face.

'It's okay, Danny,' she cooed as though she was quieting a baby. 'It's okay. I'm here. You're safe.'

Her husband's eyes flew open. They were wide and staring, like portals to another terrifying world where, even though he was awake, part of him still remained imprisoned. It was a world Liz knew he would never forget. When the shaking subsided, he looked into her eyes and sighed. She could see he was embarrassed and ashamed.

'Sorry,' he muttered, like a guilty little boy.

She looked down at him, wished she could ease his troubled mind, extirpate the images that lurked in his brain, bring back the old, carefree Danny. He had once done as much for her.

'It's not your fault,' she murmured.

'Time I was over it,' he snapped, angry at himself now. 'I feel like a coward, Liz.'

'Damn Afghanistan,' she said, then added more softly: 'You're not the only one has flashbacks. You wouldn't be human if you didn't. Time heals.'

He gave her a sideways look. 'Hope you didn't marry me because you felt sorry for me, kiddo?'

She placed the point of her finger against his temple. 'The boy I knew is still in there amongst all the rubbish. He's just been wounded in places you can't see.'

Normally, she could cheer him up, bring him out of his despair, but this time she could see he was more morose than ever.

'There's something else, something I can't tell you,' he mumbled, averting his eyes. 'It's playing on my mind, Liz. Best I go away on my own for a while, out onto the moors, think things out, decide how to handle it.'

'Go away!' she echoed, flaring up. 'Is it me, Danny? Have I done something wrong?'

Danny grasped her hand. 'Of course not! Don't think that. You're all I have in the world that's worth . . . anything.'

She forced herself to remain calm. How should she handle this? she wondered. There'd never been secrets between them and it hurt there was something he didn't feel he could share. He'd always been a man for the great outdoors, loved natural surroundings, often told her that only in the wild did he feel he could get in touch with his true self, put things in perspective. No, his wanting to be alone didn't bother her, but the idea that he couldn't confide in her did. They'd always been able to tell each other everything.

'We've never kept things from each other.'

Danny's face contorted. 'I know but . . . this is different.'

Biting her lip, she said, 'You're worrying me, now, Danny. It must be serious if you can't tell me about it.'

'It is serious,' he grunted, eyes cast downward, not able to meet hers.

Liz's heart sank. 'You're in some kind of trouble?'

He didn't answer; he turned his back, slid out of the bed, opened the curtains, stared out of the window.

'Don't worry about me,' he said, finally. 'I'm not in trouble but my so-called friends could be.'

It was a relief to hear he wasn't in trouble but her relief was tempered by the resentment she could hear in his voice. She knew loyalty to his friends meant everything to her husband, so what was going on?

'If you're not in trouble why do you have to get away?' She hesitated, then added, 'And why have they suddenly become your 'so-called' friends?'

He turned his face towards her. Framed in the window, it looked as grey and leaden as the sky she could see over his shoulders, as though dark forces were vying for his soul and he didn't know which way to turn.

'I need to get away from everybody so that I can think properly,' he said, rubbing his eyes. 'There's something I have to work out . . . a question of loyalty . . . the right thing to do.'

'Two heads are better than one. Going away on your own won't — '

Danny sliced the air with his hand, cutting her off mid-stream. The gesture was so out of character she was stunned.

'What I decide to do could affect you, Liz. I have to work it out. Do what's best for everyone.'

Even more bewildered, she could feel herself getting angry. She couldn't believe he wasn't sharing this, especially now he'd told her she was involved. Could it all be fantasy brought on by his mental traumas?

'So I'm involved, am I?' she said, her tone sarcastic.

'What affects you, affects me,' he answered as he started to pull on his shirt.

He was really irritating her now but she knew not to press him too much when he'd obviously made up his mind. He had a stubborn streak sometimes and she sensed nothing she could say was going to move him.

'I'll go to the cottage,' he said with an air of finality. 'Do my thinking there.'

Liz didn't reply, just leapt out of bed, threw on her dressing gown, flounced out of the bedroom and headed downstairs to the kitchen. In a mood, trying to work it, she started to pack his rucksack. The cottage he'd referred to was ill-equipped, an isolated place two miles off the Whitby coast road and surrounded by moorland. Danny had inherited it from an eccentric uncle who hadn't visited or looked after it in his latter years so that now it was in a dilapidated state. Danny had stayed there on occasion all the way back to boyhood, most often alone, using it as a base for the long walks he enjoyed. Liz understood from her own experiences the need he had to sometimes be alone, so she decided she wouldn't protest any more, no matter how much he was worrying her.

Ten minutes later, as she was fastening his

rucksack, he came into the kitchen dressed in his old army gear.

'Thanks for packing,' he grunted. 'I'll pick up supplies on the way.'

'You'll have breakfast before you go, won't you?'

He shook his head. 'Catch the early train if I go now.'

Liz frowned. Danny missing a meal was something else to add to her worries, a first, because he liked his food. Normally, when he was going off on a walk, or any of his outdoor pursuits, he ate the full fry.

'At least take your mobile phone this time,' she said as he turned to face her.

It was old ground. She'd tried in the past to convince him to take it with him but he always refused because he considered it a trapping of modern civilization that defeated the purpose of living with nature. His reaction was no different this time.

'Don't want anyone ringing me, interfering when I'm trying to sort out my mind.'

'My God, Danny!' she said. 'Are you sure you're not being overdramatic here? You're not that together yet, you know. Wouldn't you be better talking this out with someone . . . if you can't talk to me?'

A hurt look came into his eyes. 'You don't understand,' he said. 'Just leave me be.'

She fell silent. He had such a strong bond with his friends; what could possibly have happened where they were concerned to make him like this? And how was she involved? If he had to go away, if he couldn't tell her, it must be serious. She'd thought they could trust each other with anything and she couldn't shake off a feeling of rejection.

'One more thing,' Danny said, his jaw set. 'Don't tell anyone where I've gone, no matter what.'

She nodded agreement but was more puzzled than ever. The mystery was deepening and she was growing more concerned. What was going on in his head? Had he succumbed to paranoia brought on by his war experiences? she wondered. When she spoke, she couldn't keep the tetchiness out of her voice.

'So when will the happy wanderer return?'

'Soon as I work things out, I'll be back.'

Taking her by surprise, he reached out, took her in his arms, kissed her and whispered, 'I love you, Liz. You've got to trust me on this.'

Before she could say anything he was out the door and starting down the garden path with long, determined strides. Liz watched him go, thinking of the shy young soldier he'd been when they first met. With his caring nature and wise words, he'd been her saviour back then. Had he changed since those days? Not really, she thought. Underneath he was still the same man, except he was struggling with bad memories and frustration because he hadn't been able to find a job since leaving the forces. Her own part-time job slaving in a laundry didn't pay well and his pride was hurt that she worked while he didn't. As she closed the door, she hoped, for the sake of his health and her peace of mind, he would be able to sort out whatever was bothering him.

⋆ ⋆ ⋆

DI Alex Graham contemplated the files piled on his desk and scratched his head. They contained enough unsolved cases to keep him occupied for the foreseeable future. He knew other detectives might have complained but, while he didn't exactly relish the workload, he was happy his days would be occupied to maximum capacity.

Rising, he walked to the window, stared out at the Middlehaven Development site which was dominated by Middlesbrough's Football Stadium. The area was progressing but there were still parts unfinished. Beyond that, the iconic Transporter Bridge hovered over the River Tees like a gigantic Meccano model. The river was not polluted now, as in former days. Alex wished the same could be said of parts of Middlesbrough where the criminal elements still resisted the advance of civilization as though they were on a personal mission to set mankind back a million years. This was his town and he felt emotionally attached to the good people, wanted to catch those who blighted their lives. Yet, he knew his furious work ethic was fuelled by more than any altruism. The truth was, apart from his work, he had little else in his life. Work had been what helped him forget; if not a panacea, at least a palliative. Five years ago, he felt his world had ended, wanted it to. Now at least he was able to live with the tragedy that had damaged his life, had learned that you had to let a loved one go or live a life of continual suffering and regret.

A knock on his door interrupted those thoughts. Just as he reassumed his sitting position, it opened and a wisp of a man blew in. With his slick grey hair, pencil build and immaculate suit, his visitor looked more of an accountant but was in fact DCI Smithers, his boss. Alex groaned inwardly. When he visited it was more often than not bad news.

Smithers' gaze swept the room, landed on the files sitting on the desk.

'Busy, Alex?' he said, gesturing at the files. His eyes twinkled. 'Or just pretending, like

some around here who think I don't know it
. . . More fools them, eh!'

'What do you think, sir?'

Smithers laughed. 'Know you well enough
and your workload. In fact, I'm so aware, I'm
here to lighten your burden for a change.'

'That would be a first. Must be a catch
somewhere.'

Smithers perched himself on the edge of
the desk, patted the files. 'The Robert Walker
case, young lad found murdered on that
country road in the Cleveland Hills.'

Alex pushed a finger against his temple,
rotated it like a corkscrew. 'Believe me, that
one's burrowed deep in my brain. Just a lad,
he was.'

Smithers picked at a thread on his suit,
captured it and let it go. 'Nothing is
happening, is it, Alex?'

It was a loaded question and the DI knew
it. The young soldier had been brutally
murdered three months ago but other than
faint tyre marks at the scene, which had
yielded nothing significant, there had been no
real clue. A deluge on the night of the crime
had ensured any forensics had been washed
away. Alex found the lack of progress particularly hard to take. The lad was eighteen, the
same age his own son had been when a hit-and-
run driver had killed him on another lonely

road not that far from where they'd found the soldier's body. That needless waste of another young life had, in the detective's mind, become somehow linked with Jamie's death, acted as an extra incentive to find the killer, as though by finding justice for Robert Walker he could strike a blow for his own dead son, for all the young lives that ended tragically.

'No, sir, nothing's happening,' he said bitterly. 'We focused hard on his colleagues at the army base in Catterick but got nowhere. The lad was a bit of a loner, spent most of his life in orphanages until he joined up. Nine months later he was dead.'

Smithers stood and walked to the window. Alex followed him with his eyes, pretty sure what was coming next, hoping he was wrong.

'We'll have to scale down,' the DCI said, not turning. 'We need men elsewhere. We're at full stretch and it's been three months.' He turned to face his DI. 'I've an audit soon and can't afford to be seen wasting resources where there appears to be a dead end.'

Alex allowed his disappointment to show in his face. He'd invested so much time and energy in the Robert Walker case this was hard to take.

'I'm doing my best, sir, and I'll get there in the end,' he said.

Smithers was quiet for a moment. The DCI

was a good copper at heart. Alex knew he wouldn't be doing this lightly. As every copper knew, logistics and finance dictated everything these days.

'Come on, now, Alex. You know how it is.'

Alex nodded reluctantly. 'You're right, three months with nothing to show is no good from where you're sitting.' He sighed. 'It's just that it's become a little personal with me.'

Smithers laid a hand on his shoulder. 'That's not good but I think I can understand why. Don't take it so hard, man. The case isn't cold. You will still be able to allocate time and manpower — just not as much.'

Alex forced a smile. 'Any more good news, sir? Or is that my quota for the day?'

Smithers didn't take the sarcasm personally. He made for the door and turned to face his DI, an enigmatic smile playing on his lips, the kind that suggested he knew something he was keeping a secret for now.

'Your smile tells all, sir,' Alex said.

'Does it indeed,' the DCI replied. 'Does it tell you I'm giving you a new detective sergeant, who's due to transfer in tomorrow from the Leeds Force?'

'Can I put him to work straight off, or is he just promoted and in need of a bit of nursing along?' Alex asked.

That enigmatic smile returned fleetingly, which Alex found a little annoying. What could be so amusing about a new arrival? He figured there must be a downside, waited for the DCI to deliver a punchline which didn't come.

'Oh, I think you'll find this DS is experienced enough and knows this area pretty well,' Smithers said, adding: 'You'll rub along fine together, I'm sure.'

'Good,' Alex said, just a bit warily. What wasn't Smithers telling him? he wondered as the DCI opened the door, stepped half way out and positioned himself as though it was a shield between them, only his upper body visible.

'You might end up grateful, Alex, and not just on a professional level,' he said. 'Fortunately, I know you can keep the personal and professional apart or I wouldn't have taken the chance.'

With that parting shot Smithers shut the door, giving Alex no chance to take the matter further and leaving behind more than a whiff of mystery. He pondered it for a moment, then gave it up. What would be would be. Smithers was a strange one, hard to figure in many ways. But under that cool, practical exterior, there was a heart he didn't always show. When Alex was down and almost out, he'd been one of those who'd done what he could to help him through. That counted for a lot.

His thoughts returned to the Robert Walker case. He selected one of the files from the pile, extracted two photographs, studied them with an empty feeling in the pit of his stomach. One showed the young soldier's body lying on the edge of a single track road, the other a close up of his head. Someone had used several blows, probably with a baseball bat, to stove it in. There was no doubt the murderer intended the young man to die. Not for the first time, Alex cursed the deluge that had, fortuitously for the killer, ruined the crime scene.

He placed the photographs back in the folder, told himself that even with reduced manpower he wouldn't let the case rest. Every case counted with him but this was a personal quest. Jamie and Robert Walker were linked in his mind and he still hoped for the kind of luck that had failed to happen in Jamie's case.

★   ★   ★

Liz could hear birdsong greeting the sun's first rays as she ran along the pathway that scarred the wooded slopes of this particular part of the Cleveland Hills. Occasionally, she came here to run a route Danny had shown her, one which he and his pals used. This early there was never anybody about and she felt safe, though she was well aware Danny disapproved of her running alone.

Today though, after a sleepless night, she felt the need to burn up the miles, release those endorphins to help relieve the stress she'd been feeling since her husband had gone off to the moors two days ago in that mysterious and disturbing mindset. She hoped afterwards she'd feel a little better but didn't hold out too much hope.

The track became steeper, rising to a long ridge. In response to the incline, she shortened her stride rather than lengthening it as many inexperienced runners did, taking more out of themselves that way rather than adjusting, letting the hill have its way. Danny had taught her that, as he had so many things, saying as in life sometimes taking a step back was the right thing. She supposed in a way he was doing that now. She'd married him after his return from Afghanistan. They'd made up their mind to marry before that posting and, on his return his mind was in such a mess she considered he needed her more than ever. Time and patience would, she was sure, bring back the old, carefree Danny. Besides, he'd always been there for her, hadn't he? When she'd been a naïve 17-year-old alone in the world, working in dead-end jobs, living in dingy bedsits in a lifestyle so different from the one she'd grown up with, he had been her protector. There'd been a rare kindness in him. When he relaxed it was still there. Where would she have ended up without him? she wondered, shuddering at the thought.

The trees were sparse now. At the base of the ridge there were other tracks, one of which would merge with her own when she descended. Glancing down, she caught a movement. It must be an animal out foraging, she thought. Then she zeroed in, saw two figures dressed in black tracksuits moving along a lower track like sleek black panthers on the prowl. It gave her a start; she'd never seen anybody out here this early before. There was something about them that set off warning signals, something not quite right, out of kilter with the tranquil surroundings. Or was that just her imagination?

Deciding to obey her instinct, err on the safe side, Liz picked up her pace, hoping they wouldn't look up until she'd reached the thicker trees just ahead. But fate decreed otherwise; one of the men lifted his head and spotted her. She saw him nudge his companion. They both stared at her and even at a distance their stares felt predatory, not just born of curiosity about a lone woman running alone so early in the morning.

Their intense scrutiny seemed to last forever. Then, finally, they averted their eyes and walked on, but now at a much slower pace. They were talking animatedly, she noted, their body language suggesting that they were arguing. Wanting to leave the disturbing scenario behind, she lengthened her stride.

The ridge gradually petered out and met the lower track. Pausing to draw in a few deep breaths, she looked back nervously. There was nobody there and she felt a surge of relief. Those men hadn't retraced their steps to follow her, otherwise they'd have been in sight by now. Nevertheless, she told herself this was the last time she'd run here alone because something about those men had touched a primitive fear inside her and she knew she'd never quite feel the same sense of peace on this route ever again.

Soon she was running on much more open ground, feeling better with the expanse of blue firmament above and wide spaces of bracken on either side. She glanced over her shoulder. One more check to reassure herself.

Nothing there, thank God. She could relax now, enjoy the rest of the run. Then, just ahead, as though to mock her complacency, she saw what looked like a bundle lying at the side of the path. She told herself it must be a discarded sack but, as she came closer, it took sharper definition and another possibility thrust its way into her mind, sent a tremor of fear through her body. She slowed to a walk as she approached it. Part of her brain was telling her to stop, turn around, but her legs disobeyed and she continued towards it as though compelled.

★   ★   ★

After seeing the girl, the two men walked on to give her the impression they were going on their way but as soon as they were out of sight, they halted. Her unexpected appearance had given them a jolt and they weren't happy at all.

Frost, the taller of the two, said, 'She got a damn good look at us.'

The other one, Hurst, shrugged. 'Just a glimpse. Besides, she was on another path. She'll probably forget all about us.'

Frost gave his partner a disdainful look. 'The paths merged, you idiot, and she saw enough to describe us.' He hawked and spat.

'Should have known better than to leave the recce to you. Knew I didn't like this place . . . too open. But you insisted, nagging on about getting it done and getting home.'

'You're worrying too much,' Hurst told him. 'We'll be long gone from here before anything happens.'

Frost narrowed his eyes and, struggling to contain his anger, looked back along the path. Ten years he'd been in the game, mostly working with Hurst. Experience should have told him to check things out himself. This was to be his last job and it was his rule, as Hurst was well aware, never to leave a loose end, never mind how insignificant it might seem. The woman had seen his face, simple as, and he didn't like that one bit.

'I live a kick in the backside down the road,' he moaned. 'I don't want to be sitting in a restaurant or pub one day, happy as a cat in mint, and that woman walks in hearing memory bells. Things like that can happen . . . have happened. Prison is full of over-confident fools and my freedom is precious.'

'Come on,' Hurst said. 'It's unlikely.'

Frost prayed for patience. 'We've been successful because we cover all the bases. Why should we slack now?'

Hurst had the grace to look a little

24

shamefaced. Frost knew well enough his partner had a careless streak, didn't have the brains to imagine consequences, was one of those who thought it wouldn't happen to him, as though he had special divine protection. This in spite of the fact that both of them had witnessed men happy one minute and dying in agony the next. Hurst should know by now you had to cut the odds. Frost liked to think of himself as a perfectionist. What had just happened was far from perfect.

'I'm going back,' Frost said, face adamantine. 'You please yourself.'

'Maybe you're right,' Hurst muttered, but with little conviction.

'We've wasted enough time, sunshine. Let's get it done.'

They started to run, matching each other stride for stride, both physically fit specimens who'd trained hard ever since their younger days in the Royal Marines where they'd first met. Frost had known his partner would go along with him in the end. He also knew the real reason he hadn't wanted to go back for the woman was that he suspected his wife was having an affair. It was playing on his mind and he was obsessed with the idea of going home earlier than expected, catching her at it. There were a hundred ways of catching her out, of course, but that was his big plan. That lack of imagination again. Frost considered it a good job his partner was a crack shot and pretty nerveless in a tight situation or he would have dissolved the partnership and the sham of friendship, on his part anyway, years ago.

'It'll be another body,' Hurst chuntered as they picked up pace. 'Max might not like that.'

'Max doesn't give a damn as long as the client is satisfied and nothing gets back to him,' Frost told him. 'Besides, another body confuses the investigation for the police, doesn't it?'

★   ★   ★

For a moment, Liz couldn't move, stood there as though a cold wind had blown up from nowhere, penetrated every part of her body turning it to a block of ice. The corpse lay face down, a neat hole at the back of the head, blood trickling into blond hair like a liberal dose of jam poured onto custard. She vaguely registered the dead man must have been a jogger like herself because he was wearing shorts and a training vest not unlike Danny's.

As she gradually unfroze, she realized that

her priority was to ring the police. But her mobile was in the car; it was a good mile or so back to the car park and those men could be anywhere. The way they'd looked at her in that furtive, predatory manner, as though she'd strayed onto their territory, didn't fill her with confidence that they weren't the killers. But she knew there were no habitations anywhere near, so what else could she do but turn back? Consoling herself with the thought that they'd probably be long gone by now, she turned, started to run.

She'd only gone ten yards when they appeared on the path, moving fast in her direction. She pulled up short, heart pounding, transfixed by the two figures, as though she was watching her own death approaching and there was nothing she could do to avoid it. One of them raised his arm in a beckoning gesture. That broke the spell. Just for a moment, she wondered whether they might be coming back to help her, then realized the idea was ludicrous. The beckoning was just an enticement to get her to drop her guard. Her survival instinct kicked in. If she ran on the track, they would catch her for sure. A quick scan of the ground told her the only option was the thick wooded area thirty yards off to the left. The trees might give her a chance. Not daring to look back, she leapt into the bracken, focused on the trees, hoping they'd be her salvation.

She stumbled into the tree line, tripped. Thorns pierced her palms. She pushed herself up, ran on, glanced over her shoulder. Two shadowy figures enshrined in morning mist were not far behind her. Dreading that she would fall, she ran for the darkest part of the wood, darted behind a tree trunk, dared to look back.

The two men were standing in a clearing, their heads held high, swivelling. They reminded her of hunting dogs sniffing for a scent of their prey. Driven by panic, Liz's brain raced, skidded into dead ends as she failed to bring order to her thoughts. Then she remembered Danny telling her that a soldier in a tricky situation was trained to slow down, consider all his options rather than giving in to blind panic. She managed to calm herself enough to think logically. If she just kept going like this those two animals would surely run her to ground. Her only real chance of escape was to make for the car, use that to escape. Her sense of direction was pretty good and she thought she knew the right way. Get to the car and you'll be free! As she set off, her brain repeated those words like a mantra, blotting out negative, morale-sapping thoughts that tried to undermine her.

Her optimism was short-lived. From somewhere behind came the faint thud of a silencer followed by the zing of a bullet flying past her cheek. Pieces of bark erupted from a tree just ahead. She deviated into an even thicker, darker area of the wood, praying it would give enough cover.

Branches lacerated her face and hands as she hurled her body through the thickets, aware how easily she could fall, break a leg or ankle, be rendered helpless and at the mercy of her pursuers. She'd always hated seeing a fox chased by hounds. Now, as she gasped for air and imagined a bullet tunnelling into her back, she understood the terror of a hunted animal.

Her eyes searched for a glimpse of light. Had she wildly overestimated her capabilities, misjudged the direction? Was she merely descending further and further into a pit of darkness from which there could be no escape? The trees, like silent sentinels, seemed complicit in frustrating her efforts. And all she could see were more trees, an army gathering against her, its silence a stubborn presence mocking her folly. Then suddenly, cracking sounds broke the silence. She panicked thinking they were gunshots, then realized that it was her pursuers stepping on dry branches and that they weren't far behind her.

Alex Graham stood outside DCI Smithers' door trying to compose himself. He was never at his best early morning and what he had just observed in the car park, before he had even had a chance to take his first caffeine fix of the day, wasn't helping. When he entered the office, he found Smithers at his desk, piles of paperwork neatly arranged in front of him. Alex often wondered whether his boss's personal life was as well organized as his office. Today, though, that didn't cross his mind because he was consumed by the matter that had brought him here. He could tell by Smithers' wince when he saw his visitor's face that he knew well enough what was coming.

'I take it you've met her, then,' Smithers opened. He let the statement hang in the air for a moment before he continued. 'It's written all over your face, man, like you just had your backside slapped.'

'Not met,' Alex said, 'I saw her across the car park and someone told me she was the new DS.' In an accusatory tone, he added, 'And that's how I found out, sir.'

Smithers took it on the chin, didn't change his expression.

'Look, I know I should have told you but I

30

thought taking you off the Walker case was sufficient unto the day.' He hesitated, rubbed his chin. 'Besides, I didn't think it was exactly bad news . . . sensitive maybe, but not bad. Thought you might even like it . . . in a way.'

Alex sighed his displeasure. The DCI was straying into very personal territory here and he knew it.

'You got that one wrong, sir. I'd have liked to have had at least a chance to discuss alternatives. Right now I'm hoping it's not too late for that.'

Smithers brought his hands together, formed a steeple with his fingers. 'You needed a DS. I considered my options but in the end didn't want to disrupt other teams, decided I had enough faith in your professionalism.' He dismantled the steeple, focused on Alex, eyes like gimlets. 'Unless you can tell me it will interfere with your job, I'm afraid I have to stick with my decision.'

Alex stared into the corner of the room, tried to hide his emotions, which in truth were on a roller coaster ride, Sandra Best the reason. How should he answer? Sandra had been a young DC working with him at the time of Jamie's death. He'd been a DS then and they'd grown close . . . too close. She'd helped him through that terrible experience, enabling him to function at work when his

31

world seemed to have no meaning. Eventually though, to his eternal shame, afraid of himself, of any emotional entanglements after losing his son, he'd ended it rather cruelly. Shortly afterwards she'd transferred out and they'd parted like strangers. That had been five years ago and he hadn't heard much about her since.

When she'd appeared in the car park this morning, he thought he was seeing a ghost. Like an errant schoolboy he'd taken a circuitous route to avoid face to face contact. What was Smithers playing at? He knew how close they'd been. Was he hiding a pair of wings under that pristine suit, fancying himself as Cupid's little helper? Alex doubted it. More likely, he was being pragmatic, just as he'd indicated. Besides, he couldn't know the reasons, or the pain and turmoil involved in the break up or surely he'd have vetoed the idea. Seeing a possible way out of the situation, Alex fixed his eyes on his boss again.

'What about DS Best? Surely she's not really happy to be working with me again.'

Smithers leaned back, eyed him in somewhat of an avuncular air. 'She said she had no objection, if that was my preferred choice, said your relationship was a long time ago . . . in another lifetime.'

That stark summation of their affair took Alex by surprise, hurt him a little though he knew he had no right to feel that way. He supposed it was a small mercy, a worry halved if she thought she could work with him. What it didn't do was take into account how it might affect him. That other lifetime was more potent where he was concerned, sometimes drip fed into his present so that he had to keep it at bay. Sparked by her presence, would everything bad about that period come back to him, like a defeated enemy returning even more vengefully? He knew he was still embarrassed and guilty about the manner in which he'd ended it, the feeble excuses, avoiding her because he was afraid. His only mitigation was that he'd lost the son he'd brought up after his wife Sarah had died so young.

Smithers' voice broke through his reverie. 'Will it affect the way you do your job, Alex?'

That felt more like a challenge than a straightforward question. He'd never shirked responsibility, even when it left a bitter taste, even in those times when his inner resources were stretched to breaking point. In the big scheme of things, Sandra's return should be a minor matter. He told himself he'd handle it because he had to and because five years had passed and he should be able to.

'You know it won't,' he said, shrugging, palms upwards in a gesture that meant he surrendered. 'No way I'd let it.'

Even as he said it, he realized he wasn't as sure as he'd sounded. The DCI's smile was inscrutable. Having worked with him, he knew Smithers was a wily customer, which had probably contributed to his quick rise in the force. But he'd always liked the man, realized some of his decisions were due to constraints placed upon him by those higher up the chain, a fact that those lower down couldn't always appreciate.

'You can count on me, sir,' Alex added, meaning it. 'You earned my loyalty a long time ago.'

Smithers blushed. 'Appreciate that, Alex.'

Before either man could say more, from behind Alex a knock came on the door. Smithers, rather irritably, called for whoever it was to enter. When the door opened, Alex noticed the DCI's eyes darting over his shoulder to whoever had entered, then quickly back to him. Sensing it was probably a good moment to take his leave, he rose from his chair.

'I'll leave you to it, sir,' he said, half turning, hand resting on the desk. 'Regarding the — '

He realized there was something familiar

about the figure at the periphery of his vision, and turned right round to find himself staring into the face of Sandra Best. It was all he could do to conceal his shock. She met his gaze with a neutral expression, no sign of emotion.

For him, five years fell away in an instant. Whereas before there'd been a girlishness about her that sometimes made him feel guilty about the ten-year age gap, as though he'd been stealing away her youth, he could see she was a mature woman now with a confident air only experience could have brought.

She offered him her hand without speaking and he shook it nervously, just managing to hold her gaze while his brain scrabbled furiously for words — without success. In the end, she beat him to it.

'It's been a long time. Pleased to see you looking so well.'

He couldn't detect anything but warmth in her tone, no hint of recrimination. Her manner was purely that of an old friend. It helped put him at ease, though he was conscious of Smithers hovering at his shoulder like a maiden aunt in consort mode.

'Apparently you'll be working with me,' Alex mumbled, then realized how boorish that sounded, and tried to make up for it. 'I know how capable you are.'

With a tight little smile, she brushed past him, shook hands with the DCI. Alex didn't move as they exchanged a few pleasantries but his stomach was turning cartwheels. Finally, Smithers caught his eye, winked conspiratorially.

'I'll need to have a word with DS Best, Alex,' he said. 'Perhaps you could brief her later.'

'Of course,' Alex muttered and made for the door, grateful to be heading out of there.

As he was about to exit, Smithers called after him. 'By the way, thanks for your support.'

The DI hesitated, looked down at his feet, mumbled, 'That's okay, sir.'

Once he was outside the office, he headed for the main entrance. He wasn't in the mood to face any of his colleagues, needed a breath of air to help him clear the swirls from his head. He told himself the first meeting with Sandra hadn't gone too badly, all things considered. Working with her again was something he'd just have to accept with all the good grace he could muster. But he knew it wasn't going to be a picnic on a personal level because, in spite of their split, Sandra Best had always meant a great deal to him and, as soon as he'd laid eyes on her, he'd known not much had changed.

Liz thought she couldn't run any longer. She was sure her legs had nothing left to give and her heart was racing. Desperation was setting in. She just wanted to lie down, surrender to the nightmare behind her. Then, at her lowest ebb, she spotted a thin shaft of light lancing through the overhead canopy. That gave fresh impetus to her weary legs. She ran on, spirits rising as more beams penetrated the trees, bringing light into that dark world from which she'd thought she'd never escape. Then, suddenly, the funereal silence of the wood was broken by birdsong. She'd never heard a sweeter sound, a message of life and hope transcending the shadowy gloom. Perhaps she was going to make it after all. But that fresh burst of hope was tempered by the knowledge that those men were still behind her, that she could easily miss the car park.

Chest heaving with effort, she burst out of the tree line and could hardly believe her luck. The car park was right in front of her. Like a faithful old friend her yellow Micra was waiting there, ready to whisk her away out of this nightmare. She stifled the cry of exultation rising in her throat. Fifty yards! Fifty yards of open ground was all that lay between her and the means to freedom. She reached into her pocket, gripped her keys like a miser his last piece of gold and braced herself for one final effort, her ears and eyes straining for any sight or sound of human presence.

It was almost too quiet. Why could she no longer hear the birds singing? Had those men outflanked her? Were they lying in wait? As she hesitated, the distance to the car seemed to expand and her imagination ran riot. But what choice did she have other than to cross that clearing? If she stayed where she was they'd find her for sure. Gathering the remnants of her courage, figuring it was now or never, she fixed her eyes on the Micra and burst into the clearing at a run.

Twenty yards to go! Only twenty yards! She was already reaching out ready to press the key fob. For sure, she was going to make it. She would see Danny again, thank God. But then, as though angry at her presumption, fate played another hand and she heard men's voices, couldn't resist looking over her shoulder just as one of the men stepped out of the trees, his eyes boring across the intervening distance. Her spirits plummeted. She was a sitting target. Pure fear seemed to drain the energy from her legs, numb her brain. But she kept going, forcing the last reserves from her exhausted body.

She made it to the car, fell against it, pressed the fob, yanked the driver's door open, catapulted into the driver's seat. Her hands were shaking so much it took her three attempts to place the key in the ignition. The engine roared into life first time and she found first gear. A screech of tyres vied with her scream of relief and exultation as she rammed her foot down on the accelerator and shot off.

The scream soon died on her lips when she saw both men framed in the rear-view mirror, guns rising in their hands as they gave chase. Liz crouched low, pushed into second gear just as a hail of bullets demolished the rear windscreen. Her whole body stiffened with the expectation of another volley but before it came she hit a bend, hurled the car around it and was out of sight. The junction with the main road soon appeared. She didn't hesitate, pulled straight out into the path of a lorry, the loud blast of a horn almost welcome, given what she had left behind her.

She overtook vehicles more recklessly than a boy racer, not caring she was over the limit, wanting to put as much distance as possible between her and those men with guns. Nausea hit her in waves now that she had time to realize how near to death she'd come, but nothing could have made her stop. It wasn't that far to Middlesbrough Police Headquarters and she figured only there would she feel safe.

★ ★ ★

After his encounter with Sandra Best, Alex Graham headed straight outside, feeling the need for some fresh air and a moment of solitude. It was quite cold, too cold considering it was early May. The vagaries of the weather, Alex knew, were the cause of much complaint but mostly it was just something to talk about. The Teesside people were inured, just got on with it, regarded a continuous good spell, even in summer, as a gift rather than a given norm. He supposed it mirrored their attitude towards their lives: stoicism forged in harsh times, passed down from their progenitors in the iron and steel industry. He wished he was tougher, able to brush things aside and be optimistic, but the truth was that, other than the satisfaction derived from his work, his main aim was surviving without too much disruption to his routine and his personal life. These past five years he hadn't expected or wanted much beyond a steady rhythm to his days. He feared Sandra Best's return might threaten

40

that, make him remember the dance of life had once been more exciting and vibrant than a slow waltz.

As though in complicity with that thought, a crash of gears and discordant cough of an over-revved engine disturbed his reverie. He stared across the car park, spotted a yellow Micra shooting into a space to come to rest at an oblique angle. He figured the driver must be someone very late for work but the young woman who stumbled out was dressed in a tracksuit and trainers — hardly work attire. She sprinted to the main entrance and up the stairs. Alex was close enough to register she had scratches on her face and that her tracksuit was ripped, guessed someone else's week had started even worse than his own. A few moments later he went back inside, hoping his day would spring no more surprises. The girl racer was standing at the desk, arms gesticulating as she poured out a tale to the desk sergeant, who was looking bemused and trying to calm her down. Figuring more than likely it was a domestic complaint, Alex tried to sneak past but the sergeant spotted him and called his name.

'Problem, Sergeant?' he said, approaching the desk.

Hearing his voice, the woman turned around. This close, he saw she looked

41

exhausted and more than a little desperate.

The sergeant raised an eyebrow at him. 'Think this is one for you, sir. This lady wants to report a murder and . . . other things.' He turned back to the woman. 'This is Detective Inspector Graham.'

She stared at Alex with a glazed look that made him wonder whether she was on drugs and creating a fiction in her own mind, which would be a waste of his time. It wouldn't be the first occasion that had happened.

'I saw the body . . . they came after me . . . shot at me,' she stuttered almost as though she herself didn't believe what she was saying.

'Where was this body exactly, Miss . . . ?'

'Hunt, my name's Liz Hunt,' she snapped, as though it was a foolish question, her name an irrelevance. 'It's up in the hills. They might still be there. Please hurry.'

Something told him she was no druggy, this one, but that she was definitely in shock. Something had frightened her — badly. He needed to calm her as quickly as possible, get the facts. His eyes flicked to the sergeant.

'Get this lady a mug of tea, hot and sweet, and bring it to interview room two.' He turned to the woman again. 'It's comfortable there and you can rest while you tell me everything that happened to you.'

She didn't argue with him. A calmer, resigned look came into her eyes. As though she'd suddenly become conscious of her bedraggled appearance, she pushed back her hair. Alex took her gently by the arm and guided her down the corridor.

Interview room two was comfortable, slightly more homely than the other rooms, which was why he'd chosen it. The woman slumped down opposite him, fiddled impatiently with the zip on her tracksuit. Soon the sergeant turned up with the mug of tea Alex had requested, placed it in front of her and took his leave. She gulped it down and when she'd had her fill, sat back and stared at him.

'Go ahead, Liz,' he said. 'Tell me exactly what happened.'

'There was a body. I saw the killers. They came after me with guns.'

She was still staring at him but he could tell something was replaying in her mind, something that had embedded itself deep in her psyche and wouldn't let go. Alex had seen that disorientated look before, mainly at accidents when the survivors, surveying the carnage, realized how near they'd been to extinction and found it difficult to comprehend.

'It's over now. You're safe here,' he said. 'Try to relax and go right back to the beginning.'

Like a creature emerging from a long hibernation, she blinked rapidly, gave a shiver. Alex watched her patiently as she came to terms with the fact that whatever had happened really was behind her now and she was safe.

At last, she started her tale and he didn't interrupt, just gave an encouraging nod whenever she hesitated. When she'd finished she looked drained, pale as a corpse. Considering what she'd been through, Alex thought it was no wonder.

'Well done!' he said. 'Now we can get cracking and send our lads out to those woods.'

She made to rise, fell back again, the effort too great. Alex figured adrenaline had seen her through her ordeal but it was wearing off, leaving her exhausted.

'I'll come too,' she said. 'Give me a minute.'

'You've been through enough. Leave it to us. I'll fetch a map and you can show me where it all happened. A doctor will take care of you. There'll be more questions later and it's best you're fresh.'

She opened her mouth as though she was going to protest but seemed to think better of it. Alex rose from his chair.

'I'll fetch that map.'

'They'll be long gone,' she called out as he

headed out the door. 'Long gone!'

The first person he saw when he left the room was Sandra Best. She was standing with her back to him looking at a notice board. His first instinct was to avoid her but he'd promised Smithers he'd be professional where she was concerned, that he would handle the situation. He had things to organize quickly and she was a member of his team so the natural course would be to ask for her help. Trying to make his voice as natural-sounding as possible, he called out to her.

'Know you've just arrived and this is a fast ball but we've a probable murder case on our hands. Ready to lend a hand?'

'Of course,' she answered. 'Best to get stuck in straight away . . . it will bring me up to speed quicker.'

He explained the situation, told her to collect an ordnance survey map and take it to the interview room. He asked her to acquaint herself with Liz Hunt and to try to pinpoint the murder scene. Meanwhile, he'd inform the SOCOs they'd be needed and put armed response on standby in case those men were dumb enough to be hanging around.

'I'll be heading out there myself,' he concluded, 'so you might as well come with me since you'll likely be working on the case.'

She walked away without a word and he

sighed his relief. He'd dived into the deep end and it hadn't gone too badly. They'd fallen straight into working mode and, as long as he could maintain that practical approach, he figured he would be okay.

★   ★   ★

Alex and Sandra found the body exactly where Liz said it would be. Careful not to contaminate the area, they waited at a distance until the SOCO boys turned up, which didn't take long. Fortunately, the sun had deigned to make an appearance, though there still wasn't much warmth in the day and both were glad they'd wrapped up well. When it came to the recent weather, 'Be Prepared' wasn't just a motto for boy scouts.

The SOCOs managed to manoeuvre their vehicles up the track but it was a tight squeeze. They soon isolated the area with tape and set up a tent around the body. Alex always felt a bit of a spare part watching them going about their work, a feeling enhanced by those white suits they wore, which, coupled with their slow deliberate movements, always made him think of spacemen. Finally, one of the spacemen came in their direction and Alex fired a question at him.

'Anything you can tell me at this stage,

beside the obvious?' he asked, trying to hide his impatience.

The man shook his head. 'Other than rigor mortis hasn't long set in, nothing much. The bullet in the back of the neck killed him all right but there's nothing to help identify the corpse except for the tattoo on his forearm, which no doubt you'll have already noted.'

Alex nodded, mumbled his thanks and stepped out of the way. Liz Hunt hadn't mentioned the tattoo of a rose on the dead man's forearm. She'd probably been too shocked to even notice it and anyway why would she mention it? He turned to Sandra.

'It could take some time for them to finish up. Best we head back. I'll report to DCI Smithers and get things moving at that end.'

Sandra's eyes drifted to the woods where, according to Liz Hunt, the men had pursued her and fired guns.

'They might have left some traces in the woods and in the car park,' she said.

Alex nodded. The area needing to be examined covered a larger acreage than most crime scenes, which meant a lot of painstaking work and use of manpower.

'Already told the SOCOs that. Soon as we're back at HQ, I'll arrange for uniforms to carry out ground searches. I'll bet they'll just love that.'

Sandra frowned thoughtfully. 'This looks like a professional hit, doesn't it?'

Alex was reluctant to agree. It would make the killers much harder to catch. But the bullet in the back of the neck, the early hour and the remote location, all indicated premeditation and made it a strong possibility. One thing the killers hadn't taken into consideration was someone like Liz Hunt stumbling onto the scene. He hoped that was a mistake that might prove their undoing.

As they set off back to the car, Alex said, 'We'll need identikits of the two men from Liz Hunt. If we're lucky, she might remember something else about them once she's fully recovered.'

'If it happened the way she told us, she could still be in danger,' Sandra commented. 'They didn't chase her all that way for nothing. Must have been afraid she could describe them in some detail and it worried them.'

'If it happened the way she told us . . . ' Alex repeated back to her, smiling. 'I like that. Never make assumptions, eh?'

Sandra grinned. 'Learned that from you. Working with you when I was so young and pliable turned me into a right cynic.'

He saw her blush, knew it was because she'd realized her meaning could be extended to more than their past working relationship. It seemed to throw her literally as well as metaphorically because she almost stepped into a large puddle and he had to grab her arm.

They walked on in silence. Even though it had been just for a moment, holding her arm felt so natural, almost as though they had never been apart. He dismissed that as foolish sentiment. Parting had been the best for her because his son's death had changed everything. After the cruel way Jamie had been taken from him, he hadn't wanted any emotional entanglements, was afraid of being too close to anyone. His sole need had been to find the man responsible for Jamie's death. That need had never really gone away, though he had learned to live his life without it consuming every living minute, as it had once threatened to do. But he regretted his total selfishness, the cruel way he'd treated Sandra, the way he'd just finished it without a proper explanation. Thinking about it now made him dislike himself.

They reached the car, climbed in and set off, with Alex driving. He wanted to say something because his conscience was bothering him. After a struggle, he eventually found words.

'Look, Sandra,' he said, hands gripping the

steering wheel. 'My behaviour back then . . . it was . . . inexcusable. I wasn't coping. You didn't deserve . . . If it wasn't for you I might have gone under. I'm sorry . . . truly sorry.'

There was a long silence. He thought she wasn't going to answer, just let his words drift away into the ether in the same way as what she'd once felt for him must have.

'It was all a long time ago,' she said, at last. 'We were different people back then. No need for regrets or apologies.' She paused. 'Just treat me like the rest of your colleagues.'

He glanced at her, couldn't delude himself that he no longer had feelings for her. Five years ago he'd told himself he didn't want her young life withering along with the ruins of his own. Had he really been that noble or had he just been seeking a reason to excuse his behaviour?

'Thanks,' he said, eventually. 'Thanks for not holding it against me. Wouldn't have blamed you. It'll be good to work with you again, Sandra.'

★ ★ ★

The police doctor, an avuncular, grey-haired man in a sharp pinstriped suit, pushed a bottle of pills across the table. Liz Hunt picked the bottle up, attempted to look

50

interested by giving the label a cursory glance, then slid her gaze back to the vase of roses adorning the window sill. It was the roses that were demanding her attention, not for their beauty, or for any aesthetic reason, but because they'd triggered something in her brain that disturbed her.

Right from the moment she'd noticed the flowers, she'd been flashbacking to the body lying on the track, her vision telescoping to a forearm decorated with a single red rose. Could it be, now she was distanced from the initial horror of discovering the corpse, more details were surfacing in her mind, or that her imagination, stoked by stress, was conjuring a false memory which had no basis in reality? What really disturbed her, though, was that Danny had a tattoo just like that on his forearm.

'You're just a little bit shocked, my dear, otherwise you're fine,' the doctor was saying, his voice miles away.

She was muttering her thanks when there was a knock on the door. At the doctor's bidding, a young WPC entered, asked whether the patient was fit enough to accompany her to an interview room where DI Graham wanted her to make a statement.

'Feel up to it?' the doctor asked

She sighed, started to rise. 'The sooner it's

done, the sooner I can forget about it all.'

She followed the policewoman down the corridors to the interview room where the DI she'd seen earlier was already seated, the redheaded woman DS occupying the chair next to him. That red hair was the brightest colour in a room so dreary and drab it seemed more like a mausoleum. Grey walls, green chairs and an off-white table seemed designed to transmit depression and misery. She wondered if the ambience was deliberate, a subliminal tactic to encourage guilty interviewees to strip their stories of all pretence, get down to the stark truth.

She noticed there was more formality about the detective's manner, if not exactly a coldness, certainly less warmth than before. The inspector started proceedings, pointing at the tape recorder on the table, telling her it was there as a matter of form, that all interviews were recorded and not to worry about it. As he leaned forward to switch it on she rapped out the question she was bursting to ask, halting him mid-motion.

'Did you catch those evil bastards?'

He shook his head. 'We're on to it and will do everything we can. What will help us is your account of what happened. Don't leave anything out because sometimes even a small thing, which seems insignificant, can assume gigantic proportions looked at from another angle.'

With that, he switched on the tape recorder, announced the time and those present, asked her to recount her experience in her own words. She began but, as she continued, wondered whether she should mention the tattoo and that she thought it was like her husband's. The inspector had stressed the importance of small details but surely they must have seen it for themselves, so why bother? After all, the dead man could have no connection to Danny. Why bring her husband into this when he apparently already had enough on his plate? Though her conscience bothered her, she decided protecting her husband's privacy was her priority and decided not to mention it. Anyway, she wasn't even sure she really had seen it.

'Can't have been easy revisiting all that,' the redhead told her when she'd finished and the tape was switched off. 'Quite an ordeal you went through. You were a brave woman.'

The inspector said, 'Now all we'll need from you is an identikit of the men. Our computer has a photo database that can be searched using a description, so with your help we might hit lucky there.'

Liz said wearily, 'When I've done that can I go home?'

The detectives exchanged a meaningful look. She saw it and figured it could only mean bad news. All she wanted now was to go home as soon as possible, lie down and sleep forever. What else could they possibly want from her?

'It's not quite that simple,' the DI explained. 'You see, we're nearly certain those men were professional killers. You had a good look at them.' He eyed her steadily. 'Men like that don't take any chances, which is the reason they came after you.'

Liz's mouth went dry. The detective hadn't said it outright but the subtext was clear enough; she was still in danger. Deep down she'd suspected as much, just hadn't wanted to face it. Suddenly everything seemed as grey and joyless as that bleak room and, with a sense of pessimism, she voiced what the detective had only implied.

'My God, they could still want to kill me. That's the truth, isn't it?'

Her words hung in the air like a heavy cloud presaging a storm. The redhead avoided her gaze, stared at the grey wall as though there was something there worthy of her attention. Her colleague rubbed the bridge of his nose and took his time answering, choosing his words as though they were a rare species that needed careful nurturing.

'There's a small chance they might,' he said. 'On the up side, they'll figure you came to us, that their main opportunity has gone.'

The redhead lost whatever interest she had in the wall, tried to help him out. 'But we can't assume anything . . . for your sake. Best if we keep you safe and sound. You can see that, can't you?'

Liz slumped forward, shoulders hunching. 'I just want to go home. Surely they'll just forget about me after what's happened, concentrate on hiding.'

'Going home is not a good idea,' the redhead told her.

She wanted to defy them, march out, forget this nightmare. But her own intelligence told her these people were professionals and knew the score. However reluctant she might be, the sensible action would be to go along with them, at least for the time being.

'If I can't go home, where can I go? I need to be home for my husband.'

The DS said, 'Don't worry, your husband will be informed. He'll want you safe and sound, won't he?'

'Can you tell us where he is right now so we can contact him?' the DI added.

Liz fell silent. It was a simple enough question, but a dilemma for her. She remembered Danny's last instruction to tell nobody where he'd gone, wanted to honour it. But he couldn't have foreseen an exceptional situation like this, so what should she do? The two detectives were waiting for an answer, the silence stretching to the point of embarrassment. If she told them where Danny was, she'd be breaking her husband's trust and that meant everything to her.

'You okay, Liz?'

The DI's concerned voice interrupted the fight she was having with her conscience. She knew she couldn't delay her answer any longer, would have to appease them while honouring her husband's wish.

'My husband doesn't work. He's not long out of the army. It's hard to find work, you see. Those poor boys . . . '

She was rambling, heading into a cul-de-sac. The detectives were leaning back, watching her as though she was a child they needed to indulge for the moment.

'He's not at home right now, my Danny. He's . . . away.'

The detectives' faces didn't change. She hoped they'd put her vagueness down to stress, not deliberate subterfuge.

'Exactly where is he, Liz?' the DI asked, his tone not unkind.

She put her head down, forced strength into her voice, came back at him.

'I said he's away, didn't I?'

She realized she sounded insolent and they were sharp enough to gather it probably meant she had something to hide, but she was determined to keep Danny out of it.

'It's all right, Liz,' the DS said, 'you're not dragging him into anything . . . into danger. He'll have to be told where you are or he'll worry about you, won't he?'

'He's gone away,' she answered, even to herself sounding as though she was doing them a favour. 'I don't know where.'

The lie made her uncomfortable because she knew that one leads to another until the liar is enmeshed in a web of deceit. She excused it by telling herself this was a white lie, her motive justifiable.

'You don't know where he is?' the DI asked.

She met his gaze. There was no going back now. She'd just have to brazen it out, embellish the lie.

'He's ex-infantry, the outdoor type, even as a boy. Sometimes he just goes off on his own, needs time away from people, from towns. He comes back feeling better in himself.'

'He'll have his mobile, though?' the redhead queried.

Liz shook her head. 'He likes to keep it simple, no trappings of modern life. That was how they trained, the infantry. The last thing he wants to hear when he's away on the hills or moors is a mobile ringing. It defeats the purpose . . . in his eyes.'

The redhead frowned. 'But what if he gets into difficulties?' Liz could hear the scepticism in her voice. 'I thought all participants in outdoor pursuits carried mobiles these days. Been known to save lives, hasn't it?'

'Danny has a different mindset. I've tried to persuade him it's wise to carry one, even if just for my sake, but it's a blind spot with him.'

'A macho thing,' the DI chipped in.

She nodded. 'Probably a bit of that, more a long-standing habit.' Not quite knowing why, she added, 'It might sound selfish of him but he's a good husband.'

'But you do know when he's due back?' the DS said, pushing back a loose strand of hair.

'He's been away a week now.' Liz hesitated. 'I think he'll be back soon.'

It was another vague answer. The inspector filled his cheeks with air, let it out slowly while his colleague just stared at her.

'Have you any relatives?' the inspector inquired. 'Someone who'll put you up until we think the danger has passed?'

Lying for Danny had upset her. Unfortunately, she was going to have to lie again, this time purely for her own sake.

'None at all. Danny and I were both orphans when we married.' She grinned lopsidedly. 'Not exactly the attraction of opposites but it had the advantage of no family disapproval.'

The DI leaned his elbows on the table, cupped his chin in his hands. Liz thought his expression was not far short of incredulous.

'In that case, if you're agreeable,' he said in a measured tone, 'we'll put you in a safe house with a WPC to look after you.'

'Have I an alternative?'

'Not really, not until we know it's safe. We'll send someone to your home to pack a bag for you. As for your husband, we'll keep an eye out for his return. Meanwhile, is there anything we can get you?'

'Aside from a holiday in the Bahamas, I'd love a shower and maybe a change of clothes.'

The redhead stood up. Maybe she was imagining it, but Liz thought she detected a change in her manner, a stiffness, not the same friendliness as before. When she spoke, her matter-of-fact tone reflected that change.

'I'll show you to the showers and then we can arrange for a policewoman to collect the things you need.'

Liz followed her to the door, managed a faint smile for the DI as she was leaving the room. She was sure the smile he gave her in return was merely perfunctory.

★ ★ ★

When Sandra returned to the interview room, Alex still hadn't moved. He just stared into space as though, provided he tried hard enough, he could break through to another, parallel universe where he would find answers he was seeking. She sat down, turned towards him, raised a quizzical eyebrow.

'I wouldn't give a penny for your thoughts,' she said, 'because I think I already know what they are.'

'There was a time . . . ' he muttered, then, realizing he was about to make a sentimental reference to their past that she might not like, changed tack. 'Fair exchange is no robbery, Sandra. You go first.'

Sandra heaved a sigh. 'Well, she was so fidgety when she talked about her husband she was like a cat waiting to be fed. Not too sure I trust her after that display. Got me thinking about the rest of her story.'

'My feelings too,' he said. 'You think she's misleading us, then?'

Sandra rubbed her neck, pondered for a moment before she spoke.

'First off, she was out there running alone.

60

Not many women would do that. Secondly, she was hedging about her husband, doing her best to hide it and taking an age to answer. Why?'

'I'm wondering about that,' Alex said. 'Anything else strike you?'

'Well, you can call me a cynic, or out of tune with the modern female, perhaps, but I don't think many women would let their husbands go off alone like that without either of them knowing how to contact the other.'

Alex nodded. 'I have limited knowledge of the female psyche, as you could probably testify, but I'm with you there.'

She pushed her hand through her hair. 'Your turn now. Did I leave anything out?'

'Relatives,' he mused. 'No relatives. Hard to believe it possible in one so young. I suppose it happens, though it's stretching it for her and her husband to both be orphans. Is she hiding something from us, Sandra, do you think?' He shook his head. 'I have to say she was in genuine distress when she came in here.'

'What do you want to do, boss?'

He gave her a sharp look. Back in the day, she'd only called him boss when others were present. Had she used the term now to reiterate, in case he had other ideas, that theirs was purely a working relationship? If so, it was unnecessary.

'We have nothing solid,' he answered, 'and our number one priority is catching those killers, so we'll hang fire, give her the benefit of the doubt . . . for now, anyway.'

★ ★ ★

Hurst shuffled about in the passenger seat, for the umpteenth time glanced at Frost sitting next to him in the stationary van, willing him to end this tedium. Frost sensed his discomfiture but continued to munch his hamburger, washing each mouthful down with a sip of tea from a polystyrene cup. Eventually, he could no longer contain his irritation with his partner.

'That paper's doing no good sitting on your lap where no one outside can see it,' he chuntered. 'And while you're at it, get stuck into that kebab.'

Both were dressed in blue overalls and wearing flat caps. The idea was that anyone showing an interest would take them for workmen on a break.

'You sure this is the street?' Hurst said.

Frost sighed. 'I already told you that I gave Max her registration number. He has police contacts and they came up with this.'

Hurst made a show of looking at his watch.

'For two hours we've been driving around, shifting position, changing disguises, wasting time. I don't think she'll come.'

Frost didn't answer and Hurst continued to drone on.

'This is dangerous. Someone's going to get suspicious. Best we get out of here and forget about her. If you ask me, we should be finishing the other one off and running for home.'

Frost turned his blue eyes onto his partner, gave him a look that left him in no doubt he was tired of his complaining.

'Patience, like thinking, has never been one of your virtues, has it? I already made it clear enough that I won't give this up . . . so leave it.'

Hurst screwed his face up, stuck out his lower lip.

'Can't help wondering about my wife,' he moaned. 'You'd be the same in my position.'

'No I wouldn't,' Frost snapped. 'I'm not like you. I haven't forgotten we're professionals and professionals don't give way to emotions. You used to be a soldier, ice cool in combat, even in the desert heat. What's happened to you, man?'

'Women happened!' Hurst said, his voice drenched in bitterness. 'Been divorced twice. Don't want a third. They're leeches, women!'

'Want my advice, do you?' Frost asked, his tone long-suffering without a trace of empathy.

Hurst glared at him. 'You never married. What can you tell me?'

'Once bitten, twice shy for a start! When it's dying . . . it's dying, feller. Don't try to revive it. Move on instead. Start again. Remember that soldier you once were. Money is good but it can't buy your pride back.'

Hurst was quiet for a moment, then said, 'Different days, mate. We were told what to do back then. Life was simpler.'

'A man shapes his own ends.'

Hurst's expression was uncomprehending, childlike in a middle-aged man.

'What did you say?'

'You're an ignoramus, pal,' Frost said, sighing. 'It's a Shakespearean quote, means our own actions dictate the way our lives turn out.'

'Should have just said that, then, shouldn't he?'

Frost figured there was no answer to that and, anyway, there wasn't time for a seminar about character and fate because at that moment a police car entered the street and cruised up to the house. Frost fixed his gaze on the car with the single-minded intensity of a bird of prey, his aquiline nose enhancing the effect.

A policewoman and policeman exited the car, gave the street more than a casual once-over before they entered the house. Ten minutes later the male came out of the house carrying a suitcase, followed by the woman carrying a traveller's bag.

'The lions will lead us to the lamb,' Frost said but his meaning was lost on Hurst.

Frost drained his cup and started the engine. Hurst, smiling because at last they were going to be on the move, threw the remains of his kebab into the footwell.

'They'll take us to what they believe is a safe house,' Frost said, lips parting into a satisfied smile. 'We'll do her there . . . simple as.'

'The road is long with many a winding turn,' Hurst muttered, already back to his disconsolate self.

Frost grimaced. 'What's up with you? You trying your hand at Shakespeare now?'

'The Hollies sang that, mate.' Hurst managed a satisfied grin at what he perceived as a victory over his partner. 'Beats that Shakespeare feller any day. Means things happen in life you don't expect to.'

'Well, then, that reinforces my point, doesn't it?' Frost said. 'The woman ain't going to turn up unexpectedly in my life to bring me down. You got to minimize risk like I always have . . . for both of us.'

That seemed to shut Hurst up and Frost concentrated on the police car. He'd been trained in surveillance years ago. Using one car wasn't ideal, but he figured the coppers in the car ahead were only your average plods, probably hadn't been trained to spot a tail, at least not one of his standard. Anyway, if they'd been any good they'd have used an unmarked car instead of announcing themselves to the world. Who did they think they were dealing with here? Amateurs?

They followed the vehicle through the centre of Middlesbrough. For once Frost was happy that the traffic was heavy because it meant they were less conspicuous. He thought he'd lost them at one set of lights because they changed quickly and he didn't make it through. Letting go a volley of curses, he watched the car disappear into heavy traffic. But the driver wasn't breaking any speed limits and he soon caught up.

Frost followed the police car onto the north bound A19, stayed on its tail when it headed off into Norton Village and finally ended up following it onto a new estate. Eventually, it turned into a cul-de-sac but Frost drove straight past noting that only half the houses were completed and that they were built next to a stretch of open countryside. He made a three-point turn further on, drove back in time to observe the policewoman carrying a bag into one of the houses.

'Gotcha!' he exclaimed. 'See, she's in that one. Talk about hiding in plain sight. Piece of cake.'

Hurst's frown betrayed the fact he wasn't as pleased as his partner.

'They must be expecting us to come after her,' he grunted. 'No telling how many men they've got in there to guard her. Couldn't we just leave it?'

Frost ignored the question. He'd already made his point of view clear enough. He was pretty sure, given that most forces were struggling with manpower, the woman wouldn't have many guarding her.

'There were unfinished houses opposite,' he stated. 'No workmen around. No for sale signs up yet.'

Hurst sighed. He figured he knew where his partner was going with this. He was like a dog with a bone when he got started.

'You could set up a surveillance in the house opposite,' Frost said. 'There's plenty of countryside to use as an approach, plenty of ways for a man of your skill to get in there.'

'And you?' Hurst shot back at him. 'Where will you be when I'm in there with a builder's nail sticking into my backside?'

'I'll be putting a nail in the other guy's coffin.'

He gave Hurst a scathing look. 'It was me who did the recce so there won't be any loose ends to worry about . . . not this time.'

That shut Hurst up. A weary sigh his only protest, he opened the passenger door and climbed out.

'Anything happens, get on your mobile,' Frost told him.

Hurst leaned back into the car. 'Good job we're retiring,' he said. 'I'm getting too old for larks like this and so are you.'

Frost watched his partner in the rear-view mirror until he disappeared. Hurst could follow orders, would be all right, do his job in spite of his protestations. When he'd taken care of the other piece of business, they'd have to decide on a way of killing the woman. It would be their last kill and, in a way, he was sorry it had to be her. She'd been a warrior out there in the woods, better than a lot of men. It was simply a case of needs must, maintaining standards.

★   ★   ★

Billy Hall stared at his artificial hand. He supposed, if it was possible to be objective, ignore the fact the surface was so smooth and pristine, it was a good enough simulation of a real hand, a flesh and blood hand. People often remarked that it was lifelike. He accepted that kind of comment with a nod of the head and a forced smile. But those words only enhanced his awareness that it was different. The trouble was he couldn't be objective. With his innate shyness, he hated being noticed and the hand felt like an appendage, not a real part of himself, not part of the man he'd been before Afghanistan.

A glass of whisky sat on the table in front of him. Enshrined in a ray of sunlight lancing through the kitchen window, it was gleaming like a little amber god . . . so innocent, so innocuous in appearance. But Billy knew its power, the grip it exerted on his life. Sometimes it felt like his best friend. At other times, which were becoming more frequent, it was a worse enemy than the Taliban had ever been. Even now, it was whispering seductively that it could help him and he was more than ready.

His eye alighted on the tattoo on his forearm. Its juxtaposition with his false hand was for him a constant, ironic comment on his life. It had been a foolishness of his youth meant to symbolize a unity and a camaraderie that would last forever. But all that feeling had evaporated now. His false hand was a reminder of his false hopes, his self-deceptions before his eyes had opened to how things really were in the world.

A tear born of frustration ran down his cheek. His good hand started to slide towards the glass. He withdrew it as though from a hot flame, forced himself to think about his pal Jack Peters, who was having to cope with two missing legs. Shouldn't he consider himself lucky it was just his hand? When the bomb had gone off, he'd been thrown clear of the vehicle and had crawled into a ditch. Jack had been trapped inside crying out in agony, so he'd gone back for him, hauled him out and carried him back to the ditch. He had emerged from the episode unscathed except for the sniper's bullet that had ruined his hand, that and the mental scars only too manifest in his subsequent nightmares.

He'd been lauded as a hero at the time but he'd come to detest the fact he'd allowed the medal and the praise to massage his ego, seduce him into believing he was strong enough to cope with his handicap. Civilian life soon taught him the brutal truth. People at home didn't care enough, didn't really understand Afghanistan, doubted the army should even be there. He had come to consider his hand had been sacrificed on the altar of ignorance and indifference.

His glance shifted to the newspaper lying next to the glass. It was open at the jobs page but there were only a few vacancies. What chance did he stand with his disability when the able-bodied were finding it a struggle to find work? His compensation and pension were a boon but not enough. He was only thirty-five, for heaven's sake, and his wife was out there working right now in a job she hated. He loved his wife. Why should she suffer because of him?

The amber tempter glinted and he could no longer resist its overtures. His hand snaked out, lifted the glass in one swoop. He hurled the liquid into his mouth, relished the burning sensation in his throat. His pal John came into his head, that idea he'd had for making them some money. At first he'd balked at it, but as his prospects seemed to diminish with every passing day, its appeal had grown proportionately until he'd agreed. In just a few days, they'd be splitting sixty grand. They'd send ten grand to Jack, which left twenty-five thousand each, enough to start a small business, the kind where one hand wouldn't be a handicap and he might be able to recapture his pride. The man they were taking it from could well afford it and, all told, he was getting off lightly. Unless he was guilty as sin he wouldn't have agreed to pay up, would he? The whisky and the thought of the money coming to him lifted Billy's mood.

He'd started on his third glass when he heard the knock at the front door. Pushing himself up with his good hand, he swayed until he found his balance. Surprised at how much the drink had affected him, he leaned on the wall for support as he made his way down the hallway. His fingers and the key seemed at war with each other as he tried to insert the key in the lock. He fumbled and cursed until they harmonized and he hit the target. An old habit, a residue of the pride in the soldier he'd once been, made him straighten as he turned the key and opened up.

Billy's heavy-lidded gaze roamed over the tall man framed in the doorway, taking in the blue overalls, gloved hands, the bag he carried, the flat cap, the badge hanging around his neck, which made him think of his own useless medal. His gaze narrowed eventually to the face and two eyes staring at him from either side of a hooked nose. Billy didn't like those eyes, didn't know whether it was the coldness he thought he saw in them or the wind gusting through the open door that made him shiver.

'It's too cold . . . for c-c-cold calling,' he slurred, giggling at his own joke.

Taking his badge between fingers and thumb, his visitor held it towards Billy, who gave it a cursory, blurry-eyed glance.

'Advance and be identified,' he hiccupped.

'I'm not the enemy, Mr Hall,' the man said, smiling. 'I've come to read your electric meter.'

'Some people read boo . . . ksh,' Billy slurred, standing aside. 'Some read elec . . . trish meters.'

The man smiled again as he stepped past him. Billy closed the door, followed him down the hallway, almost careered into his back when he suddenly halted. Just managing to retain his balance, he saw the man reach into his bag, extract something dark and metallic. When he swung round, Billy wasn't so far gone that he didn't recognize it was a gun in his hand. The silencer attached to it pointed at him like an accusing finger.

Maybe it was the effect of the whisky but Billy didn't panic. He just thought that it would be typical of his luck if, after surviving the Taliban, he was killed in his own home by a meter man, that perhaps fate had realized its mistake leaving him alive, was about to redress the balance, end his misery. Yet, in spite of that, pure instinct made him step back and he twisted and stumbled, ended up face down on the floor. In the second before the bullet bored into the back of his neck Billy saw a vision of himself as a young soldier in the gym, hammering away at a punch bag, both his hands flesh and blood.

Frost turned the bag inside out, dropped the gun into it. Next, he took off the badge, overalls and cap, and put them in the bag. Then, stepping over the corpse, he opened the door and exited Billy Hall's home. As he knew it would be from his recce, the street was quiet at this time of day so he walked quickly down the path, and the few hundred yards to the town centre and lost himself in the crowds, satisfied that, if anybody had seen him leave, the blond wig and make-up he was wearing would make it impossible for them to give an accurate description.

★   ★   ★

A feeling of professional satisfaction accompanied Frost as he drove back to the housing estate in the growing darkness. He parked up at a distance, approached the half-finished building opposite the safe house from the back way, slipped through the empty doorframe. Stepping carefully over planks and debris, he called out Hurst's name, heard him answer from upstairs.

Two pieces of chipboard were propped up against the bedroom window, a narrow gap left between them just wide enough to see through. Hurst was seated on a trestle. Hunched like a gorilla, he was peering through the narrow gap. Frost's first thought was that he hoped his partner hadn't placed the boards like that because an alert copper could easily notice they'd been moved and become suspicious. When his partner turned he must have seen his dubious expression, was quick to reassure him.

'Don't worry, that's exactly how they were arranged when I came up here. How did you get on? Since you're back, I take it our man's deceased.'

Frost nodded, couldn't hide a sneer. 'I did my recce properly so it was easy. Question is, have you seen anything?'

'Nothing if you don't count mice, rats and spiders.' Hurst rubbed his legs, gave him a pained look. 'You still think it's a good idea to set up here? It might be days before anything happens.'

Frost's expression was long-suffering. 'Back in the day, you laid in a ditch for hours with just a bottle to urinate in. It was just a corporal's pay then and you didn't moan half as much. Spoiled now, you are.' He sighed. 'I don't like the risk any more than you do but it was you who made it necessary. More fool me for killing the guy in that wood when I wasn't happy with the location any more than I am with this one.'

'I'm tired,' Hurst complained as though he hadn't heard one word.

Frost said wearily, 'We get well paid, don't we? And after this we're done for good.'

Hurst shook his head. 'We can't be here too long. It's too dangerous.'

Frost didn't fancy spending too much time in that draughty hole either and harping Hurst was testing his patience. It was a wonder, really, that he'd managed to stick him all these years.

'If she's in there, I'm pretty sure something will happen soon,' he said.

Hurst sniffed. 'Never knew you to rely on clairvoyance.'

'That girl's not the type to sit on her hands.'

'You sound as though you admire her, mate.'

'Not admire . . . respect is a better word. I haven't forgotten the way she led us a dance in that wood.'

While they were talking, a solitary street lamp burst into life, bathed the room in an unearthly, yellow glow. Frost shivered involuntarily.

'No need for both of us to be here,' he said. 'You go off and get a meal. Come back in about three hours unless you hear from me first. And don't worry. We'll get our chance if we're patient.'

Not needing a second bidding, Hurst rose and stretched. Frost threw him the keys to the van, told him where he'd find it and that, when he returned, he should bring a sleeping bag and a flask of coffee with him.

Hurst made for the door, halted there for a moment.

'Talking of the past, one time we'd have just gone straight in and shot her.'

Frost didn't even bother to look at him, or to hide the contempt in his voice.

'If there's police in there and we had to kill one of them, they'd never stop looking for us, would they? As it stands I'm reluctant to kill her in this location because it won't be easy to get out of this estate and away without bringing the law down on our heads.' He sighed. 'It might be a case of needs must, though.'

As he positioned himself on the trestle, Frost heard his partner's hollow footsteps echoing on the uncarpeted stairs and then fading into the silence of the empty building. His mind started to wander and he found himself thinking about the families who would occupy this room in the future. He reckoned, like most people, only a few of them would escape what he considered a life of drudgery, the nine-to-five mundane working day that would never have done for him. Life was far too short to settle for that; you had to make the best of it, grab what you could while you were able to. He supposed, if the dice had landed differently, he might have been a business mogul, a premier league footballer, a pop star, perhaps. It just so happened those weren't his talents. Fate had decreed the best way for him to make money was by killing people. That was his business and it had been the misfortune of the woman across the street to stumble into his world.

★　★　★

Alex Graham fought off his tiredness. He'd been setting up an incident room, allocating tasks, briefing his team, everything needed to get an investigation moving; he was only too aware that those first twenty-four hours of a murder investigation were more often than not vital. Just when he'd thought he was

78

getting on top of it, another murder had been reported, one he was sure was linked to the first one, and he'd had to make adjustments to accommodate both investigations.

Janet Hall, one of the murdered men's wives, was sitting opposite him. She was a fair-skinned blonde but right now her pallor was more chalk-white than fair, more like a zombie's in one of those old black and white horror films. Tear tracks scored her cheeks and she hadn't finished crying because he could see one loitering in the corner of her eye ready to follow the others. She'd crossed her arms, wrapped them around herself, as though by adopting that posture she could shut out the world, protect herself from any more hurt.

Alex guessed she was in her late twenties and he found himself feeling desperately sorry for her. Nothing was more certain than her grief was genuine, deep in her soul. That had been obvious to him from the moment she'd entered the room. Despite the late hour, he'd sent for Sandra Best, figuring a woman was needed. Sandra was sitting beside the widow, a comforting arm around Janet's shoulder. It was she who took the initiative.

'It's Janet, isn't it?'

'Janet Hall,' the woman answered almost in a whisper.

'Are you up to answering a few questions, Janet? We know it will be hard but it's important and it will help us.'

Eyelids fluttering like a fledgling's wings, Janet turned to the DS. She looked so vague, Alex wasn't sure she'd be able to concentrate long enough to answer his questions. But she surprised him.

'Why Billy?' she suddenly groaned, her voice unnaturally deep for her small frame. 'He'd suffered enough in his life.'

'Janet, we — '

Sandra never finished her sentence because Janet Hall interrupted, her face transforming into a mask of hatred.

'I want whoever did it to suffer for doing that to my Billy,' she hissed, eyes wild as she struck the table with both fists.

'He will,' Alex told her. 'Believe me, he will. It's our job to make sure he does.'

The pure animal hatred gradually melted away from the widow's face and only her surfeit of grief remained. Alex couldn't imagine how horrific it must have been for her to return home from work and find her husband lying dead in the hallway, a bullet in the back of his neck. He'd taken the call telling him about Billy Hall two hours ago just as he was settling to his supper and a glass of wine. The SOCO boys were already at the Halls' home. He guessed, given it was the second murder they'd had to deal with, they would be calling it a roaring trade.

'You've been strong,' Sandra told the widow. 'Billy would be proud of you. He was a soldier, your Billy, wasn't he?'

The woman made an effort to straighten her shoulders, nodded at the DS. Alex took the opportunity to slide a photograph across the table.

'Could you look at that, please?' Sandra said. 'It was on your mantelpiece, wasn't it?'

As though she needed time to digest what she'd been asked to do, then co-ordinate body and brain, Janet took an age to lean forward and examine the photograph.

'We'd like to know who this is,' Sandra told her, pointing to one figure in a row of uniformed men.

'It's John . . . ' she mumbled. 'Billy's army pal . . . John Boyle.' She moved her finger along the line. 'That's Jack Peters, the one my husband lost his hand saving.' She added tearfully, 'He got a medal for that, my Billy.'

Alex allowed himself a little optimism. This was a definite breakthrough because Janet Hall had just identified the dead man in the woods as John Boyle, a pal of her husband. It could well be, then, that both men had been killed by the same man or men.

'Were they still in contact, John and your husband?'

Janet Hall turned to him with a wistful look, again took her time answering.

'They'd dreamed up some scheme together,' she said eventually, in a low monotone. 'Billy wouldn't tell me about it but said it would bring some money in.' She closed her eyes for a moment before she continued. 'He was always trying to think of ways of making money, my Billy . . . felt he was letting me down . . . not working.' She paused, hid her face in her hands, the finality of her husband's death hitting her full force. 'I just wanted him to be well in his mind.'

Sandra went round the table, put an arm around her shoulders, gave Alex a meaningful look that told him she considered the widow had had enough. But she'd opened an avenue for him and he couldn't resist another question.

'You've no idea what their scheme was?'

'No!' she declared with surprising force. 'He drank too much after he lost his hand and I was just happy his mind was occupied by something else. I didn't care about money. I cared about him and now he's gone.'

Sandra was glaring a reprimand in his direction. Janet Hall was obviously a good, loyal wife and it was time to leave the poor woman alone. He had to be pleased with what she'd given them so far. The fact that the dead men had a money-making scheme in prospect, which Billy wouldn't reveal to his wife, gave good grounds for suspicion. Had that scheme something to do with why they were killed?

'Sorry to put you through that, Janet,' he said. 'You've been very brave and a big help. Your sister will have arrived by now. The DS here will take you to her.'

Watching the widow leave the room, Sandra's arm around her shoulder, Alex felt desperately sorry for her. He knew how she felt. Jamie's death had been a bolt out of the blue, just as her husband's had been for her. Both lives had been taken by another human being, though beast would be a more appropriate description in his view. She would always resent that and it would be hard for her to live with it. She'd ask herself a million times how anybody could be so evil without even coming close to an answer. Better minds than hers or his had tried and failed to find one and going down that road in the wake of Jamie's death had nearly driven him mad.

Turning his mind back to matters at hand, he studied the photograph again. Judging by the uniforms the men were wearing, all of them belonged to the Yorkshire Regiment. The regiment's badge was a white rose and so that explained similar tattoos discovered on the dead men's arms. Was it more than coincidence that Robert Walker had been a member of the same regiment? He doubted it. That young man's murder had been totally different, much more amateurish, more like a crime of passion than anything, so he doubted there was any connection.

Sandra, re-entering the room, broke into his thought pattern. Rubbing the tiredness out of her eyes, she gave a long, woeful sigh.

'Poor woman. Her sister told me she was struggling to hold the marriage together after her husband lost his hand. According to her, if she hadn't been so long-suffering he'd have gone under. The alcohol was gradually getting a stranglehold, changing a good man.'

'In sickness and in health,' Alex mused aloud.

She shot him a quizzical look. 'You remember that bit, then.'

'Of course I do. Easy to say, harder to do!'

Sandra gave a twisted smile. 'But it's important . . . loyalty . . . Marriage apart, you find your true friends when the chips are down.'

Alex winced inwardly. Was she trying to tell him that he hadn't been as good a friend to her as she had been to him in his hour of need? If that was it, then he couldn't disagree. He felt his conscience biting hard so he tried to slide the conversation in another direction to hide it.

'I thought you'd have married by now, Sandra . . . had kids. You'd be a good mother, I'm sure.'

The minute he said it, he regretted it. He'd sounded far too patronizing. Here she was, one day in, and he'd strayed onto personal territory after vowing to keep their relationship professional. It didn't augur at all well for their future and, when she took her time answering, he was afraid she'd taken offence and would lambaste him for his crassness.

'I've been wined and dined,' she said, eventually, 'and nearly made it to the altar once . . . but we weren't suited, really.' She shrugged. 'It's not something I worry about. I've got my job and what will be, will be.'

He was relieved she'd taken it so well. Despite her stoic words, he thought she'd sounded sad.

'So you're a fatalist, then?'

She tilted her head a little to the side, produced the faintest of smiles.

'Oh, I don't know about that. Sometimes I've been known to manipulate, give fate a little shove.'

She stifled a yawn and Alex realized she

must be as tired as he was, would suffer for it the next day. He glanced at his watch, saw that it was coming up to midnight.

'Thanks for coming back in,' he said. 'I've asked a lot of you before you've even had a chance to settle in and you've been a big help. It's been a real baptism of fire but I promise I'll make it up to you when things ease off.'

Sandra shrugged. 'No problem. I haven't known a day like this for a long time but it's the job, isn't it? What's on the agenda tomorrow? Can't be any more murder and mayhem, surely?'

Alex pointed to the photograph. 'The regiment those men belonged to is based at Catterick Camp. I want more background, knowledge about any mutual friends, any enemies, that kind of thing. After tomorrow's briefing I'll see DCI Smithers then take a trip to the barracks. Since you're right up to speed, you might as well come with me. In what is a predominantly male environment, the soldiers might open up more to a female, be less on their guard.'

Sandra nodded. 'Suits me as long as they don't send me on a route march.'

'The briefing will be at 8.30 a.m.,' Alex told her. 'We might have some forensics to help us by then but I doubt it. They don't move quickly.'

'What about the media? You going to give them the full story?'

'Most of it. We're going to need all the help we can get from the public on this one . . . especially since we don't know whether those killers have finished their dirty work.'

Sandra stood up, stretched languidly and started towards the door. 'Need my beauty sleep,' she said. 'Time you were on your way home too. You look shattered.'

He made an expansive gesture with his hands. 'This is me at home.'

When she'd gone, he gazed around the room, realized that last statement was near the truth. His flat was really just the place he ate, slept and watched television before he returned to the treadmill again.

★ ★ ★

Liz Hunt sat bolt upright on the bed, stifled the cry rising in her throat, stared wide-eyed at the unfamiliar four walls without a clue as to her whereabouts but relieved that she wasn't in any immediate danger. Her ordeal in the woods came back to her and she realized that was the reason for those nightmarish visions that had haunted her sleep, those branches reaching out like dead men's arms to drag her down, the looming

87

presence of faceless men with guns. Thank goodness it was behind her. Or was it because now she remembered she was sequestered in this safe house because those men with guns might want her dead?

Danny! Her husband leapt into her mind. If only he were here beside her now. If only she could talk to him. She was glad she hadn't betrayed him but uncomfortable that she'd had to lie to the detectives. Had she really seen a tattoo like Danny's on the dead man's arm or was it a mere figment of her imagination?

A noise coming from downstairs caused her a moment of panic until she recalled they'd put a policewoman in the house with her, a pleasant enough young woman called Sheila who'd done her best to put her at ease. The faint aroma of fried bacon, evoking a semblance of normality, tempted her out of her bed. Slipping into her dressing gown, she made her way to the bathroom, showered, combed her hair and made her way downstairs.

Sheila was standing at the kitchen sink. She heard Liz enter and turned towards her looking a little wary, like a mother not quite sure of her child's mood. Liz wondered whether she'd been selected for the job because someone thought her rosy-cheeked, maternal appearance was reassuring.

'There's a bacon butty keeping warm in the oven, love,' she told Liz, 'and coffee in the pot. Give me second and I'll serve it up.'

Liz manufactured a smile, sat at the table. The policewoman fussed around, then placed the food on the table and sat down opposite her charge who, not at all in the mood for anyone's company, would have preferred to eat alone.

The conversation was pleasant enough but in the situation it seemed so banal and inconsequential Liz's nerves were soon screaming out for sanctuary. Afraid she might surrender to an irrational impulse to slap the woman's face to shut her up, she decided it was too excruciating for her to continue listening any longer.

'If you don't mind, I think I'll have my coffee in the other room,' she said, demolishing the remnants of the bacon butty in one go.

'Of course, dear! Please feel free. There's a television through there and some magazines. We try to make these places just like home, you know.'

That last remark was so naïve and patronizing it grated. This was nothing like home! Liz resisted asking her how she would like to wake up in a strange house with a policewoman she didn't know for a breakfast companion chatting away inanely, while she, her life on hold, was worrying about her husband who was out on the moors going through a crisis. Then there was the small matter of the threat to her life. Instead of exploding, she managed to force a sickly smile, then picked up her coffee and took it through to the living room.

Sitting down on the wooden-framed sofa, she wondered about Sheila's idea of a home. The word was a definite misnomer applied here; the furnishings were purely functional and the room boasted not an ounce of individuality. It reminded her of her child-hood — all those army houses she'd lived in that had seemed like clones of each other. That was why she'd vowed any home she made would carry her own stamp.

Glancing at the clock on the mantelpiece, she thought she might catch the local news and switched the television on. A newscaster was speculating about the motives of a schoolboy who had gone on a gun rampage, which didn't help ease her current state of mind so she picked up a magazine and flipped through the pages while she waited for it to finish. The magazine contained mainly trivia about celebrities and didn't hold her interest, so she gave up and threw it on the floor.

At last, the local northeast news came on. A familiar newsreader, his face suitably doleful, started to talk about a murder and when the picture changed from the studio to an exterior location, Liz recognized the spot where she'd discovered the body and recoiled as though she'd been struck an invisible blow. Then the picture flashed briefly to a house festooned with yellow police tape and the newsreader announced a second murder. Though the two deaths were in separate locations, the police thought they might well involve the same person or persons. The murdered men had been named as Billy Hall and John Boyle, both ex-members of the armed forces. DI Alex Graham of Middlesbrough Police was heading the investigation and any member of the public who might have seen something, or thought they knew something, should ring the number on the screen.

Numb and disorientated, Liz switched off and sank back on the sofa. Yesterday's horrors started to repeat in her head all over again but with a more sinister and terrifying dimension because both men mentioned were pals of her husband. She recalled Danny telling her he had to get away from his friends. All kinds of possibilities raced through her head. Perhaps someone was hunting Danny and his friends and, for some reason, he couldn't go to the police, had chosen to hide instead. The thought terrified her.

She couldn't keep still, leapt to her feet, paced the room like a caged animal, trying to decide what she should do now and finally concluding there was only one course of action open to her. Her priority was to go to her husband, find out from him exactly what was going on. They could go to the police together and that way she wouldn't feel she'd betrayed him.

★　★　★

The incident room was packed with bodies. DCI Smithers was in overall control and when he finished his motivational speech he called Alex to the front. The DI could almost smell the enthusiasm in his audience. It wasn't often there were two suspected professional killers on their territory and finding the perpetrators would provide a real challenge for everybody.

Alex brought them all up to speed on the current information they'd gathered about the dead men. John Boyle lived alone, seemed to have formed few relationships so they'd need to dig harder there. Janet Hall was providing them with information about her husband's life; so far there was nothing untoward. The teams in the hills had found boot prints around the body, bits of fibre in the trees. Bullets taken from both corpses had been sent for analysis and it was expected, but not certain, they would match each other.

Alex moved on to the allocated tasks for the day, dividing his personnel between the two murders, stressing that it was highly likely they were linked. That made it doubly important to stick to procedure, enter everything in the book so that no overlaps were missed.

When he finished and the team was dispersing, Smithers called him over for a word. Though outwardly he was showing no sign, Alex knew that underneath the calm surface the DCI must be anxious about the double whammy sitting on his plate, on both their plates, in fact. It was sure to engender a torrent of publicity.

'DI Johnson's back from his holidays,' he told Alex, 'so I've brought him in to share the work load. You, of course, remain the senior investigating officer in charge.'

Johnson was a no-nonsense Scotsman who didn't suffer fools gladly and wouldn't let his ego get in the way of teamwork; the type that probably deserved promotion but whose very strengths might frighten those above him.

Alex could work with him because he trusted him. Right now, working on two murders, he needed his help.

'That's fine, sir. I've briefed the media as you agreed. We're hoping the public might respond.'

'Anything else cooking?'

'Myself and DS Best are taking a run to Catterick Garrison. Both men were based there nine months ago and the regiment is still in situ. We might be able to pick up background details from officers and men that will eventually lead somewhere.'

Smithers blew out his cheeks. 'Any ideas about this business?'

'Not yet, sir. Could be a grudge . . . or a drug deal gone wrong, I suppose. It's early days. Maybe someone at the regiment will light our way.'

The conversation ended with Smithers saying he was right behind him. Alex, about to exit the room, bumped into the burly DI Johnson. They shook hands and Alex led him away to his office, briefed him there. When the Scotsman left, he picked up the phone, rang the adjutant at Catterick, told him he was coming down and gave an approximate arrival time. Then, he rang Sandra Best's extension, asked her to meet him in the car park.

As soon as he put the phone down, a doubt crept in. Was he doing the right thing taking her with him? Initially, he couldn't have envisaged spending a few minutes in her company without feeling embarrassed and, he had to admit, a little ashamed. Working together again yesterday had felt so natural he'd had no qualms about asking her to accompany him today. He hoped his decision had been taken for professional reasons, not old feelings that should be dead and buried but at work in his subconscious mind. He was no psychologist but understood how easily humans deceived themselves about their motives. Some criminals he knew did it all the time, actually came to believe the lies they told.

Ten minutes later he was driving down the A19, Sandra in the passenger seat. Their conversation was stilted; there were long periods of silence. She'd told him about the flat she'd bought in Nunthorpe, an up-market part of Middlesbrough, how she had considered buying a dog for company but decided a flat wasn't suitable and her hours too unpredictable. After that, neither said much until a road sign to Catterick appeared.

'Seems like only yesterday I was down here,' Alex commented. 'Visiting the same regiment, at the same barracks.'

Sandra gave a little laugh. 'Let me guess — you were doing a sponsored assault course?'

Alex grinned. 'The furthest thing from my mind but I'm glad you think I'm still capable!' His face grew serious. 'No, it was another murder case made me venture this far south.'

She detected his melancholy tone. 'A bad one, I take it.'

'Eighteen-year-old soldier, same regiment as our dead duo, beaten to death in a lonely moorland spot, possibly with a baseball bat. We never found who did it.' Alex sighed. 'It rankles, believe me it rankles.'

'Sounds just like . . . '

Sandra strangled her words, then obviously embarrassed, bowed her head like a penitent.

Turning towards her, Alex noticed her cheeks were flushed. He thought he knew the reason.

'He was murdered no more than a few miles from where Jamie was . . . struck down, if that's what you were thinking.'

After a period of silence, she said, 'Sorry. That wasn't very sensitive of me, was it?'

Alex shook his head. 'No need to apologize. He shouldn't be forgotten.'

'I have fond memories of your Jamie,' she responded, her voice tentative.

Alex sighed. 'I'll never get over it, but these days at least I can talk about him without going to pieces.'

He was conscious the past was right there in the car with them, a silent passenger, distant but watchful.

'Over the years,' Sandra said, 'I've come to understand how deeply you suffered. I thought I knew, but I was too young to realize the full extent of your suffering. How immature that was.'

He didn't know how to respond, so said nothing, let it drift and soon they were driving into Catterick, the military town that had housed generations of troops. Alex remembered his own great-grandfather had been one of them on his way to the horrors of the First World War trenches. The three murdered men had lived here too, but they had met their deaths, not for an honorable cause in some foreign field, but needlessly. Alex hoped this visit would be fruitful, better than his last one, which had led precisely nowhere.

He stopped the car at the barrier at the entrance to the barracks. A smart young soldier stepped out of the guard room, politely asked them their business. Both detectives showed their ID and Alex told him the adjutant knew of their visit. The soldier went back inside, soon returned and told them he'd been instructed to show them where to park and escort them to the office.

★ ★ ★

The adjutant was a fair-haired young man with cut-glass looks. As he rose to greet them, hand extended and exuding an air of confidence beyond his years, he conveyed an impression that he had everything within his purview under control. This was their second meeting and Alex remembered he wasn't short on charm, wondered how much was affectation, how much the real man. From his experience of many he'd encountered in his own profession, he knew too well a smart uniform and polished manner could hide a weak character.

'Ah, Detective Inspector Graham, I'm Captain Fitzroy Smith,' the adjutant said breezily, 'but then we've already met, haven't we?' In a more somber tone, he added, 'Once again the circumstances are most distressing.'

Alex introduced Sandra and the three exchanged meaningless pleasantries until eventually the adjutant pointed to a door at the other side of his office. A brass nameplate read Lt. Col. F. Martin.

'I do apologize.' The captain waved his hand flamboyantly. 'We're running a trifle

98

late. Major Tranter's in with the colonel. I'm sure he won't be too long.' He glanced at his watch histrionically. 'Wonder if you'd mind waiting here in my office. I've an errand to run for the colonel.'

'Not at all,' Alex told him, thinking he was a shade too old to be a message boy, running what he termed 'errands'.

When they were alone, Sandra sat in a vacant chair while Alex stood with his hands behind his back studying a huge picture of a cavalry charge, all blood and thunder, adorning one wall. Suddenly, as though a battle were taking place much closer to home, the sound of raised voices issued from behind the colonel's door. As the voices grew in volume, the detectives looked at one another in surprise.

A moment's silence followed the storm, then the door flew open and a rather rotund man stormed out, pent up fury emanating from his whole being like steam from a pressure cooker. With only a curt nod to acknowledge the detectives' presence, he strode across the room and out the other door as though he had an urgent need to get away from there as fast as his feet would carry his corpulent frame.

'Heard the one about the galloping major?' Alex grunted.

Before Sandra could come back with a quip, the colonel poked his head through the doorway, asked them to enter. Inside the office, he offered them chairs facing his desk. Once they were all seated, Alex reminded the colonel they'd met before when he'd conducted the Robert Walker inquiry and introduced Sandra. Though at first he'd looked slightly ruffled by that altercation with the major, the soldier seemed to have quickly recovered his composure.

'Major Tranter and I had words,' he grunted. 'I do hope he wasn't impolite to you on his way out.'

Alex gave a little smile, shook his head. He remembered his previous impression of this man. Then, as now, he'd seemed a near stereotype of a commanding officer, ramrod straight, grey hair neatly combed lending him an air of distinction. He also remembered, other than a perfunctory expression of regret, he hadn't shown much emotion concerning Robert Walker's death. Back then, he thought he'd detected a cold streak in the man, wondered whether, in his profession, he'd seen so many die in tragic circumstances he'd become inured to death. On the other hand, perhaps he was a practitioner of the stiff upper lip, one of those who kept such a tight rein on their emotions you never knew what they were really feeling.

'My adjutant outlined the reason for this second visit,' the colonel opened. 'Must say, it's rather a sad business, two of our old soldiers dying like that, and following so closely the other young man's death. But the former had both left us and were civilians, so I don't think we can help you.'

That last sentence hit a nerve with Alex. They'd barely started and already the officer was trying to distance himself and his regiment. He knew the reason; the army didn't like bad publicity of any kind. You couldn't be sure how far, or in which direction, shrapnel would travel when a grenade exploded, how far-reaching the damage and it was the same with bad publicity. If it reached up the chain of command someone would suffer and this colonel was protecting his position. It was selfish because any intelligent man could conceive that an incitement to murder might well lie in the past, perhaps something that occurred during the dead men's service years. Doing his best to hide his displeasure, Alex reached into his briefcase, extracted two photographs and spread them on the table in front of the colonel.

'Do you know these men, Colonel?'

The colonel leaned forward, gave the photographs a cursory inspection in a way

101

that suggested it pained him to do so.

'Of course, I do.'

'Well, then, you'll know they are the men who were murdered yesterday. We're pretty sure it was by the same killer . . . or killers.'

The colonel looked straight into Alex's eyes, a bit too long and a bit too intensely, the detective thought, as though he was so accustomed to exerting his will he was finding it hard to hold back whatever it was he was thinking.

'I'm not sure what you want from me, Inspector, but may I suggest that once they'd left us they could easily have become involved with the criminal fraternity. It happens to ex-soldiers, you know, when a void opens in their lives.'

'That's the first thing that springs to mind, isn't it?' Alex said. 'But in our job, as I'm sure in yours, it can be dangerous to make assumptions. If we're wrong it wastes so much time, not to mention resources.'

The colonel gave an insouciant shrug. To Alex it seemed a rude and dismissive action he'd have expected from a low-life criminal, ill-befitting someone who was supposed to be an officer and gentleman.

'So how can the army help the police?' the colonel said, with only a fraction more enthusiasm in his voice than his manner portrayed.

Alex gestured in Sandra's direction. So far, she had simply watched the proceedings, though he had no doubt she'd been forming her own opinion of the colonel, which she'd share with him later.

'My DS and I would like to look at the murdered men's records, assuming you have them, also talk to anybody who is likely to remember them — that would include all ranks.'

'My adjutant deals with matters like that,' the colonel said curtly. 'I suggest one of you speaks to the officers, the other one to the men. As it happens Major Tranter was their last company commander. You should speak to him, though I doubt he'll know anything that will help.'

The colonel sat back in a manner that implied he'd said his piece and wanted them out of his hair. It made Alex bristle. They were talking about murdered men whom he had commanded not so long ago, but he was being dismissive, as though he was talking about missing toilet rolls with his quartermaster rather than flesh and blood human beings who'd served under him. Alex decided he was going to dig his heels in.

'And you, Colonel,' he ventured, 'what can you tell us? I believe they served a number of years. Good leaders make a point of knowing all their men so you must have formed an impression.' He hesitated a fraction, stroked his chin. 'Surely?'

Aware from the detective's sarcastic tone that he was being played, the colonel glowered, shifted his eyes to the window. He stared out at the rows of barrack blocks then hauled his eyes back to Alex.

'True, I did command them,' he said, quite coolly. 'As far as I was concerned they were average soldiers, didn't stand out, particularly. Don't know too much about their individual personalities.' Suddenly, the coolness dissipated and he became more vehement. 'I'm not one of your touchy feely brigade, Inspector. Contrary to what appears to be a trend in today's army, I believe you should preserve a certain distance from the men you command. That way you don't lose that authority which is paramount in the battle situation.'

It sounded like a textbook talking. Alex wasn't too surprised, had expected as much from this man, though he had to concede there was more than a little truth in the view he'd expressed. The trouble was it could be taken too far leading to a loss of respect from those you led.

'Authority and respect, Colonel . . . two different things, aren't they? Best to have both, eh? Sometimes 'touchy feely', as you put it, earns respect and loyalty.'

The soldier's face coloured. Alex could see he was struggling to hold his temper. Probably not many people talked back to him and he was used to having the last word. He seemed to be ready to explode, then to think better of it. Without deigning to reply, he reached for the phone, rang through to the adjutant and instructed him to arrange for the detectives to see Hall and Boyle's army records and to set up interviews with officers and men they'd served with. That done, he put down the phone with more force than was necessary.

Alex decided there was nothing more to be gained here and it was time to be on their way. He thanked the colonel in as polite a manner as he could manage, then he and Sandra headed for the door.

'I doubt you'll get anywhere,' the soldier called after him. 'The regiment is a family of brothers. They don't turn on each other.'

Alex smiled. 'You're obviously not aware that a high proportion of murder cases occur in families, my dear fellow.'

He hesitated on the threshold, winked at Sandra and followed that with another shot.

'Billy — Corporal Hall — only had one hand. Did you know that, Colonel?'

The soldier squared his shoulders and ran

a hand through his hair like a rake.

'Of course!'

'Decorated for bravery, I believe.'

'That's . . . correct.'

Alex feigned a bemused expression, as near an impersonation of Detective Columbo as he could manage.

'Must be a common thing in your world . . . a man losing his hand. You probably just forgot to mention Billy was a bit of a hero.' He slanted his head, tapped his temple with his finger, Columbo style again. 'Easy to do, I suppose, when you have to preserve that distance from the men.'

It was a bullet aimed right at the heart and the colonel's mouth dropped open. Alex gave a little wave and ushered Sandra out of the room and back into the adjutant's office, shutting the door behind him.

'Peter Falk had nothing on you,' Sandra whispered in reference to the actor who played Columbo.

'You noticed . . . must have been good, then,' he said. 'Any time they want to do a remake I'm available. Got the raincoat, too.'

The adjutant looked up from his desk. If nothing else, he was efficient, already had the murdered men's files laid out on the desk for them. Alex asked Sandra to go through their files, and then interview the men who knew them. Meanwhile he'd talk to the officers. The adjutant made arrangements over the phone while Sandra moved to a desk in the corner of the room and started on the files.

'Your transport won't be long,' the adjutant told Alex when he'd put down the phone. 'The lady can work here and a vehicle and driver will be available for her when she's done.'

'Appreciated,' Alex said.

He was always impressed by the army's efficiency. In his own profession, sometimes even in such vital matters as forensics, the wheels ground far too slowly for his liking. He supposed the reason for the difference was that the army had to be constantly on the alert for war, while detecting murder was usually a much slower, abstruse affair.

After a few minutes, the adjutant said he'd have to leave them alone again and excused himself. When he'd gone Sandra looked up, met Alex's eyes and pointed at the colonel's door with a mischievous grin.

'Forgotten how sarcastic you could be when you put your mind to it.'

'Lowest form of wit,' Alex told her. 'But with old starchypants in there I couldn't help it. Apart from the obvious cold front, something about him didn't sit right with me. Last time we crossed paths was when that young soldier was murdered. His indifference was jaw-dropping, made me wonder whether he was a vampire needing a blood infusion.'

Sandra tapped her teeth with her pencil. 'I didn't hear him mention Robert Walker by name, or ask how that investigation was going.'

'Not a word passed his lips. I was going to bring it up but decided to leave it. Can't understand why he didn't. Probably too self-centred to be bothered much about the lower ranks, that one.'

'Yes, I agree and you made it quite clear how much you approved of his attitude.'

Alex sighed. 'I can't imagine him inspiring his men.'

Sandra grinned impishly. 'Talking about the men, how is it I get the lower ranks and you get the officers?'

''Cos I talk posher than what you do, my dear.'

'Not to mention there are more lower ranks, so my list of interviewees is longer than yours.'

'Never entered my mind.'

Their repartee ended abruptly when the adjutant bounced back into the office all bright-eyed and bushy-tailed, like a spaniel excited at the prospect of a hunt. Swagger stick under his arm, he glanced at his watch.

'Your transport is outside now,' he told Alex. 'May I be so bold as to suggest you meet the lady in the officers' mess at 1400 hours. After that, if you need more time, it can be arranged.'

'That'll be just tickety boo,' Alex said and turned to Sandra. 'See you later, then, DS Best. Watch your p's and q's, now.'

She shot him a withering look as he made for the door.

★ ★ ★

As he was driven through the barracks, Alex was impressed by the brisk and purposeful manner of the soldiers he saw going about their business. He didn't think many of his uniformed colleagues could stand comparison in fitness and appearance. But again he didn't need to remind himself top show wasn't everything. Plenty of murderers and rapists on first acquaintance behaved like proper gentlemen until a little digging exposed the grubby character beneath the façade. He'd seen evil residing in magnificent houses, compassion and nobility shown by people in the worst of situations.

The next couple of hours were spent interviewing two lieutenants and a captain. Until he informed them that the conversation would remain strictly confidential, each showed a marked reluctance to open up to him. The picture of the dead men that finally emerged was of good soldiers turned cynical after the Afghanistan tour and for all the usual reasons: sub-standard equipment; long hours in the field because of manpower shortage; the ignorance and indifference of public and politicians. However, Hall and Boyle maintained their professionalism until the end and nobody had noticed any enmity towards them, or any intimation of a feud that might have led to their deaths. Major Tranter, whom Alex was on his way to interview in the officers' mess, became his last hope of finding anything idiosyncratic in their lives.

Sitting in a high-backed leather chair in the anteroom, the major appeared much less florid, but flabbier and older than in that glimpse of him exploding out of the colonel's office. As he rose to greet Alex, the loose flesh under his chin wobbled, a characteristic that made him seem the antithesis of the other soldiers the detective had already met. Was it the privilege of rank, or a streak of rebel in him that allowed him to carry that excess weight when all around him seemed so slim and sleek?

'Must apologize for my behaviour earlier,'

the major said, looking a little shamefaced.

Alex feigned polite ignorance. If he said nothing, perhaps the major might elaborate and that would get him talking, be a good warm-up to the main business.

'That damn man. I swear I could swing for him!' the soldier fulminated, bringing his fist down on the leather armrest. He pouted his lips and the protruding flesh was like purple grapes. Clearly the man still hadn't fully recovered from the clash with his superior.

The major's difficulty controlling his feelings about the colonel piqued Alex's interest. His was the first real show of emotion amongst those he'd interviewed and encouraged him to hope that, if there was anything to reveal, this could be the man who would cast indiscretion to the wind.

'I take it you and the commanding officer have your differences from time to time,' the detective said, with deliberate understatement.

'You heard us in his office, didn't you?' the major snorted. 'That was one battle in the war, Inspector.'

'I heard raised voices but obviously didn't know what it was all about. Sounded serious, though.'

'Well, it's my daughter's graduation this Saturday,' the major explained irritably, 'and I damn well have to sit on an audit board. Asked him for the weekend off, since it's special, and he tells me to get my priorities right . . . the pipsqueak.' The major was so frustrated he was close to tears. 'I babysat for him when we were young officers, more fool me!'

The man was a talker, apparently not too inhibited or bound by loyalty when it came to the colonel. Alex decided to keep the conversation on the same theme, then slip in his other questions. He leaned forward, lowered his voice as though they were confidants.

'Know how you feel. Same in my job. Doesn't do anything for morale having a boss like that, does it?'

The major's frustration came out in a long sigh. 'The man makes no allowances for family life. It's army first and last with him. Promotion is all that he's bothered about, that next step up the ladder . . . doesn't care what he does to get it.'

'Sounds as though he has no family life himself or he'd understand.'

'First wife died young. Second marriage is one of convenience, if you ask me. Oh, they attend functions together and she plays the colonel's lady with the wives, but I think it's all show. Pretty much lead separate lives.'

'A marriage of mutual convenience, then.'

The major nodded, glanced towards the door, aware he was stepping over the line, not wanting anyone to hear. His revelations had been interesting, but would he have anything equally forthright to say about the murdered men? That was key and Alex decided, now the man was in his stride, it was time to find out.

'You know the purpose of my visit, don't you, Major Tranter?'

'Yes, the colonel's gopher, Fitzroy Smith, told me what happened to Hall and Boyle. I knew both men pretty well. They were good soldiers.'

The major's gaze floated away to a corner of the room. From his haunted look, Alex thought he was remembering times and places seared into his memory.

'Billy Hall lost a hand, didn't he, Major?'

Tranter's eyes darted back to the DI. His body gave a little jerk as though, after slipping away for a moment, his spirit had re-entered his body.

'He was a brave lad. He lost that hand rescuing his mate.'

The major seemed emotional, his reaction more empathetic than the colonel's had been.

'I'd heard about that,' Alex said. 'But not the details.'

'It shouldn't have happened, Inspector. We were short of men, see, but new arrivals were due. Major Martin, as the colonel was then, couldn't wait, increased the patrols. The men were already fatigued and we were pushing into unexplored territory. A mine went off and we were ambushed. Corporal Peters lost his legs, Corporal Hall his hand rescuing him.'

'So the colonel was to blame, was he?'

The major gave a twisted smile. 'Not officially. I was a captain then, his second in command. You had to be right there on the spot to understand the whole picture.'

'The men,' Alex said. 'What did they think?'

The major took his time considering the question before he spoke.

'Some of the men might have put two and two together but, in a situation that ebbed and flowed constantly, it would be nigh on impossible to prove negligence. Higher up the chain, they might have even considered that he was showing initiative, getting on with the job, keeping the Taliban on the move.'

A melancholy silence settled on the two men. The careless act that had caused his own son's unnecessary death swarmed around in Alex's mind as he spoke.

'I don't suppose you know anything that might have caused Hall and Boyle's murders, do you?'

The major shrugged. 'All I can say is that

Afghanistan changes everybody. Who knows what it stirred up in their minds? Like others, they were more cynical when we returned, that much was obvious. We tried to separate the old sweats from the new men as much as possible in case it rubbed off and lowered morale.'

'Away from men like Robert Walker?'

'Yes, I suppose. But it was an impossible task. There were inevitably times when the newer recruits and long servers came together professionally and socially.'

Alex scratched his head. 'So they would have known each other . . . Hall, Boyle and Walker?'

A gleam of understanding came into the major's eyes and his face lit up like a fat, smiling Buddha's.

'Surely you don't think their deaths are connected?' His imagination got to work. 'Oh, my! How his nibs would like that . . . the publicity.'

Alex brought him back to earth. 'There's nothing at all to suggest it. But we don't want to rule anything out at this stage, either.'

The major gestured towards the big bay window. 'Out there a different world lies in wait for all retired soldiers. Too many end up jobless, homeless or in prison. If you ask me, the odds are the men found it hard to cope, got into something they shouldn't have and paid with their lives.'

Framed in the window, black clouds were starting to gather, dark invaders of the skies intent on creating mischief. Alex had to concede the major's version could well be right but he was hoping for something more solid.

'I agree it's the most likely scenario.'

The major nodded. He seemed much calmer now. Alex thought, in his frustration with the commanding officer, he'd needed a sounding board and he'd arrived at the right moment to provide one. Later, when he'd had time to reflect, would he regret being so free with his criticisms?

'Afraid I haven't been much help,' Tranter said. 'Went off on a tangent about his nibs, didn't I? Sorry about that.'

Alex stood up, walked over to the window, noticed a Land Rover approaching the building.

'Don't worry. I appreciate your honesty, Major. Wish everybody was as forthcoming.'

The Land Rover drew up in front of the mess and Sandra Best stepped out. Alex wondered whether she'd found anybody as voluble as the major. When, a minute later, she entered the anteroom clutching a magazine, he sensed she had something to tell him but wouldn't do so in the major's presence.

'So he's your boss, is he?' the major asked Sandra, winking playfully after he'd introduced them. 'I hope he isn't a tyrant like my boss.'

Sandra grinned coquettishly. 'That's a bit disloyal for a soldier serving Queen and Country, Major Tranter.'

Her comment made him blush but he recovered when her warm smile made it evident she was joking.

'We soldiers always respect the rank, my dear . . . if not the man. That way you can tell yourself you've kept your dignity while having to obey a fool.'

'We're not exempt from that ourselves,' Alex told him, trying to maintain the commonality he'd established. 'Plenty of fools on top of our ladder trying to cut away the rungs beneath us.'

The major glanced at the door, puffed out his cheeks. 'That man down the road isn't finished climbing. He's aiming at brigadier. Making all the right noises, too.'

Alex grinned ruefully. 'Didn't you forget to say trampling on any one who gets in his way?'

The major sighed. 'Must stop going on. It's just that my daughter will be disappointed that I can't attend her graduation.'

'The young can cope. I'm sure she'll understand.' Alex held out his hand. 'I've taken enough of your time, Major Tranter.'

The major shook both their hands, told them to wait while he arranged for them to be picked up. Alex didn't know quite what to make of him, but was grateful for the information he'd provided, even though he was well aware it might prove to have no relevance whatsoever.

★   ★   ★

As soon as Major Tranter left them, Alex turned to Sandra.

'Come on, then, out with it. Soon as you walked in I could see you were bursting to tell.'

The DS grinned and held up the magazine. 'A picture speaks louder than words and you have to see what I found.'

She opened it up, flicked through the pages. When she found what she was seeking, she handed it to Alex.

'I didn't get all that much from the interviews but I did find this regimental magazine lying around in the corporals' mess. They produce one every few months, apparently. Just take a look at that picture.'

He shot her a quizzical glance, then

118

focused on the page. Below a caption which read, 'Last pints for old sweats, soon to become civvies,' was a photograph of three soldiers in uniform sitting at a table with beers in front of them. He recognized two of the men instantly. The last time he'd seen Billy Hall and John Boyle was in the mortuary when he'd made a brief visit to the pathologist. In this picture, they were brought back to life for him, smiling into the camera as though they hadn't a care in the world, blissfully unaware the angel of death had them marked for a premature end. He couldn't see anything to be excited about.

'Well spotted,' he said, hiding his disappointment. 'But this only shows they were pals and we already know that, don't we?'

'You're underestimating my powers of detection here, boss,' Sandra said and grinned mischievously. 'Hate to sound patronizing but take another look and maybe you'll see it.'

Doing what he was told, he transferred his gaze to the third person in the picture and read the name in the small print underneath. He felt a cold slither in his stomach, understood immediately why Sandra had been so fired up. His eyes came alive with curiosity as he looked at his DS.

'Liz Hunt told us her husband was recently out of the army,' he said, stroking his chin thoughtfully. 'The third guy in the picture is called Hunt. It's not that common a name, is it?'

She made a told-you-so face. 'If you're thinking coincidence, I can tell you his name's Danny and he had a girlfriend nobody ever saw. He never talked much about her or brought her to any functions. Even his friends began to doubt she existed until they heard he'd married shortly after leaving the army.'

'Well, well! You little ferret,' Alex exclaimed, face lighting up. 'Doesn't leave a lot of room for doubt, does it?'

He started to wonder about Liz Hunt and why her husband was so secretive about her. Sandra leaned across him, so close he could smell her perfume, flipped through the pages of the magazine until she came to another photograph, jabbed a finger at it.

'Try that one for dessert.'

The picture was entitled, 'Corporal Hall shows new boy the ropes'. It showed Billy on a steep rock face, demonstrating a manoeuvre to another soldier, whose face was mostly hidden. But the name printed underneath left no doubt who the pupil was and Alex felt that cold slither in his stomach again. Billy Hall and Robert Walker must surely have known each other pretty well to be in such close proximity on a rock face.

'Good work,' he told Sandra. 'It probably doesn't mean a lot but you never know. We'll keep it in mind. Our main priority now is to find Danny Hunt. He could be the only one of the trio still alive . . . we hope.'

It was all very tantalizing. Liz Hunt was the one who discovered John Boyle's body and now it turned out that he was a friend of her husband, as was Billy Hall. The hit men had gone after her and, when questioned, she couldn't, or perhaps wouldn't, tell them her husband's whereabouts. It raised questions about her and the story she'd told. Was she being entirely truthful? Did she know more than she was saying?

'We need to talk to Liz Hunt,' Alex said, as their transport drew up outside the mess window. 'Soon as possible.'

★　★　★

When, out of courtesy, they'd gone to the colonel's office to tell him they were leaving, they were told he was off camp performing an official duty and wouldn't be back in the office until the following morning. Sandra joked that he was merely avoiding Alex's sarcastic tongue.

Soon they were back on the A19, heading back to Teesside. Over in the west the sun was going down. Bathed in a hazy, golden glow, the fields seemed mysterious and dreamlike, as though a hidden hand was at work in creation. Alex's thoughts turned to Jamie. Was there a place in the universe where he would meet his son again, the intervening years apart being nothing in the great scheme of things? Or was there nothing there but what the eyes could see? He supposed, in the end, it came down to hope and faith. Today, when he'd seen that picture of Robert Walker, there'd been a moment he'd thought perhaps a hidden hand really was at work.

He figured Sandra must be wondering why he was so quiet, thought he'd better say something and so glanced across at her

'You had your suspicions about Liz Hunt's story. What do you think now, Sandra?'

She stared out of the window, across the faint golden glow of light rolling back across the fields, to the horizon where the sun was recalling the last remnants of daylight to the dark side.

'I'm wondering whether she's covering up for her husband. Aren't you?'

'Danny could be involved in those murders and perhaps she knows that,' Alex mused. 'Maybe they cooked up a story between them — or she's using her initiative — to divert our attention elsewhere.'

Sandra sighed. 'If that's so, she put on a good performance, Oscar-winning stuff.'

'Do you think it's possible her husband would kill his two pals, his comrades at arms in Afghanistan?'

She shot him a quizzical glance. 'Come on, Alex, even close friends can fall out big time. And everybody has secrets. A wife and a husband don't know everything about each other, either.'

Alex couldn't disagree. One case he covered, a man shot his wife because she failed to say good morning. To the whole outside world they'd had a perfect relationship. Bigamists he'd come across juggled two homes for years, undiscovered. He thought it no wonder policemen developed a cynical streak.

'I'm trying to think where Robert Walker comes into it,' he said, as they reached the outskirts of Middlesbrough.

Sandra shrugged, cocked an eyebrow. 'Don't push that too hard or you might see what you want to see. Just keep a little distance.'

He could see the sense in what she'd said, but it didn't mean, given the merest sniff, he would be any less diligent in pursuing Robert's killer. He'd made that promise to himself and he'd keep it.

'When do you want to question her ladyship?' Sandra queried.

He glanced at his watch. It had been a long day, it was getting late and they were both tired. If Liz Hunt was protecting her husband, he didn't suppose she'd break easily; they'd have to be cute, at their sharpest, to wheedle the truth out of her. He decided to allow common sense to prevail over enthusiasm.

'We'll have a go at her in the morning,' he said, stifling a yawn. 'You head home and get a good night's sleep. You deserve it. You did a great job today.'

Five minutes later, he dropped her in the HQ car park and watched her walk to her car. She'd been easy company again and she really had done an excellent job. He wished he was heading home with her as in the old days but remonstrated with himself for that thought. Those days were dead and gone; fate had decreed they weren't meant to be. Like that sunset dying on the fields, nothing of beauty went on forever and you had to accept that, get on with life as best you could.

★   ★   ★

Back in the safe house, Liz picked her mobile phone out of her bag. The number of the taxi firm she used habitually was programmed in.

All she had to do was press the relevant button. It seemed so easy, but she was in so much turmoil she lingered, trying to convince herself she was doing the right thing, gearing herself up to escape. Of course, the easy thing would be to tell the police Billy and John were Danny's friends, let them deal with it. She could justify doing that with those killers after her, her own life at risk. Yet, though she was tempted, she knew she couldn't do it for the simple reason that Danny had asked her to tell nobody and it would be anathema for her to break faith with her husband.

She remembered those days when she'd first met Danny. She'd been a naïve 17-year-old and he'd become her rock, never given her the slightest cause to doubt or distrust him. When her father discovered the relationship, he'd gone ballistic, ordered her not to see him again, which naturally made her more determined to continue to do so.

She started to pace the bedroom like a caged animal, then, settling herself down, turned off the bedroom light, peeked through the curtains at the street. Most houses were unoccupied, she noticed, which would help. The moon was almost full but armies of clouds were on the move obscuring it for short periods. She recalled it had been on a night like this she'd run away from home and never returned. She'd gone straight to Danny, who'd found her a place and supported her until she'd found a job miles away from home. He'd shown her so much kindness; she'd known he was the one for her. Even when he'd been posted down south, he'd come to visit her every week. Then, like an evil ogre in a fairy tale, the monster that was Afghanistan had dragged him away from her, sunk its claws into his soul, returned him to her almost broken. Gradually, thank God, under her tender ministrations the invisible wounds healed and the old Danny started to re-emerge, those uncharacteristic flashes of temper becoming a rarity.

A series of clouds moved across the moon in quick succession. Was it possible that Danny had changed and she just couldn't see it? Judging from their last conversation, something was wrong in his life. But she wouldn't allow herself to entertain the idea that he had deliberately become involved in something illegal. Once she faced him, looked deep into his eyes and heard his explanation, she was sure she would understand and that everything would be all right. For that to happen, she had to get out of this suffocating house, get him alone. The police might not like it but, for her, the only choice was to go and find him.

Steeling herself, she dialled the taxi firm and arranged to be picked up. Then she opened the window, reached out and grasped the drainpipe. Hoping her gym work would pay off and her arms would be strong enough to hold on, she swung her body out of the window, scrambled with her feet until they found purchase on the wall. Conscious that, if she slipped, she'd likely break an arm or leg and put an end to her plans, she worked her way carefully to the ground.

* * *

Hurst hadn't long taken over from Frost, his second stint watching the safe house. Already he was bored. Vigils like this wouldn't have bothered him so much when he was young but now they had begun to tax his patience to the limit. A bitter taste came into his mouth when he recalled the last time he'd kept watch. That time it had been a personal matter, worth the time invested because the suspicions he'd harboured about his wife had been confirmed; the bitch, as he'd suspected, had been sneaking around behind his back seeing another man. She must really have believed he'd gone soft in his old age not to consider the consequences of her little trysts. Or was it she thought she was too clever, and he was too thick to pick up the signs? He supposed it was true enough that the easy life had softened him up, but he was still the same man inside as he'd always been. She would find out soon enough that she shouldn't have dared to cross him. Frost thought he was anxious to return home to catch her at it, but that wasn't it at all. He had other plans.

As he was dreaming of his plan for revenge on his wife and her lover, the light in the bedroom window of the safe house went out. A moment later his attention was riveted on the woman standing at the same window in the dark. Through his binos, he watched her look up and down the street, sensed from her body language she was up to something. He was proved right when she opened the window and, with only the slightest hesitation, climbed onto the drainpipe and started to shin down. Instinctively, Hurst slid his hand inside his jacket, curled his fingers around his gun. He thought he could bring her down but remembered Frost had said there was only one way off the estate, that the police could easily trap them in the area, and he decided it would be too risky. Frustrated, he could only watch impotently as the target hit the ground, walked quickly away from the house and out of sight.

It was a totally unexpected turn of events. Hurst was wondering what he should do next when it came to him her actions could prove advantageous. There was only one road out of the estate and she had to be making for the exit that led onto the main road. If he hurried, he might be able to get there first, gain an opportunity to kill her and hide the body somewhere it would be difficult to find. That thought in mind, he didn't waste time, was soon down the stairs and out of the house. Using the field, rather than following her directly, he made it to the main road in a matter of minutes. Hidden in the bushes at the corner of the field, he had a clear view of the exit road no more than a hundred yards away. There was no sign of the woman and he hoped he hadn't lost her.

That fear proved unfounded because she suddenly appeared and stood on the corner in a state of obvious high agitation. Hurst was tempted to walk right up to her and just do her on the spot, but thought a better idea would be to bring her back to the field and shoot her down there, then hide the body in the bushes. That way there would be little chance of anyone witnessing the act and she'd lie undetected in the field while he and Frost were making their merry way south.

He made up his mind that was the way to

go, so he stepped over the fence and started towards her at a pace that wouldn't arouse suspicion, managed to get halfway there before she saw him coming. Though she kept watching nervously, she didn't move away. Now . . . if only his luck would hold . . .

The distance narrowed to thirty yards. Hurst's confidence he could pull it off grew with every step until the sound of a car's engine coming along the road behind him planted the seed of a doubt. He didn't dare turn around and the car's headlights soon bathed him in light and lit up the path where he was walking. From the sound of the engine, he could tell it was slowing down. The hairs on the back of his neck started to prickle and it took all his restraint not to turn around. Had he been set up? Was the woman perhaps a policewoman in disguise acting as the proverbial tethered goat to draw the predator into the open?

Those imaginings evaporated when a taxi drove past. He sighed his relief and thought he was back on track again until the woman stepped into the road and beckoned to the driver. The taxi pulled in beside her and the door opened. Hurst stopped walking and let out a disappointed growl when his quarry jumped into the vehicle and shut the door behind her. As the taxi accelerated into the night, he had enough presence of mind to make a mental note of the number plate and the firm. Then he got straight on to Frost on his mobile, reported what had happened and that the woman had used up two more of her nine lives. Frost told him to wait where he was and he'd be along soon to pick him up.

Frost hadn't much to say as he drove away from the estate into Norton Village. Hurst felt his silence implied his partner thought he'd messed up and he resented it. That assumed air of superiority of his was becoming more of a habit and he was tired of putting up with it. When he'd respected him, he'd accepted it, played along because he recognized that Frost was the organizer, the one with the business head. But now that he had no respect for him, it was galling to continue in his accustomed role of junior partner, playing dumber than he was.

'Maybe it's better she's cut herself loose,' Frost said, eventually. 'It means when we find her there'll be no law in our way.'

He pulled into a spot with a view of the village duck pond. In the middle of the pond, an illuminated fountain spouted silvery water like a starburst. Frost sat still saying nothing, just staring at the cascading water as though fascinated while Hurst wondered what was going on in his head, what he was going to come up with next. Finally, Hurst lost patience.

'She could have gone anywhere.'

Frost cocked an eyebrow. 'Then we need to narrow it down, don't we, pal?'

Hurst's heart sank. He'd hoped, given this latest setback, Frost might consider giving up.

'Easier said than done,' he grumbled. 'She could be a hundred miles away.'

'At least you had the wit to get the name of the taxi firm,' Frost snapped back at him, 'and the number plate.'

'Yeah, sure, but what good is that, really? She's long gone, mate.'

Frost just smiled that superior smile of his that got right up Hurst's nose, looked at his watch and produced his mobile. His eyes flickered briefly to his partner.

'Listen and learn, my friend.'

Frost rang directory inquiries, procured the taxi firm's telephone number, then dialed it.

Hurst heard a gruff, bored, male voice at the other end of the phone say, 'Station Taxis,' as though it was big effort and he was doing the caller a favour.

'Wonder if you could be so good as to help me,' Frost stated, his voice softer than usual. 'I'm nearly out of my mind with worry. You see my niece was seen getting in one of your taxis around 7.30 p.m. in the Norton area.

132

She's a heroin addict. We were trying to wean her off it but she's run away and we're worried sick.' His voice changed so that he was almost pleading now. 'Do you think you could possibly find out where she was dropped off? Is there a way?'

Hurst had to stop himself laughing. He had to admit Frost was putting on a good performance and it appeared to be working because the voice that came back was definitely a shade less lugubrious.

'Give me a second, mate.'

Frost shot Hurst a smug smile while they waited. It took a minute for the voice to return.

'Someone called Hunt booked a taxi around that time. Her destination was down as The Sailor Inn. That's out on the moorland road near Staithes, mate. Bit of a desolate spot for a young girl alone.'

'That's her,' Frost said, investing his voice with optimism. 'Bless you, sir. That's such a help.'

'Something else,' the voice continued. 'I was on the radio to the driver. He said she wasn't going to the inn, but to some cottage nearby, though there ain't much of anything around there. He was a bit concerned because it was dark, like.'

Frost smiled to himself. 'Don't worry, we

know where she's headed. We'll bring her back safe. Ever so grateful to you.'

The call ended with the guy wishing Frost luck.

'See? Even the dull and ignorant can be flattered and cajoled by treating them with respect,' Frost said.

Hurst shrugged nonchalantly. 'We might as well go to South America and look for Lord Lucan if you ask me.'

'Don't think it'll be that difficult,' Frost said, reaching into the driver's-side pocket for a map. 'You remember maps, don't you, an old soldier like you?'

He snapped the light on, spread the map on his knees. Hurst hoped he wouldn't find what he was looking for and would have to give it up, but it wasn't to be.

'There's only one building on the map within reasonable walking distance of the inn,' he said triumphantly. 'It's a fair bet that she headed there.'

Hurst raised his eyes to the heavens. 'Don't tell me — we're going on a night march now. To find a needle in a haystack!'

Frost started the engine. 'It's a good spot for a kill. In fact, it couldn't be better.'

★　★　★

Half an hour later they were parked in a lay-by at the top of a steep declivity. A building stood at the bottom with the sign, The Sailor Inn, swinging in the wind. Off to their left, the east, a stretch of open ground gave way to cliffs barely discernible in the dark. Beyond the cliffs, moonlight glittered like silver lying on the sea, gradually tapering to a point where it dropped over the horizon. Hurst noticed a cluster of lights behind them, guessed that was the fishing port of Staithes where Captain James Cook had spent a period as an apprentice before heading for Whitby and then the world. He figured the sailor could easily have stood on those cliffs dreaming of lands that lay beyond, dreams which would later become a reality for him. Not long now and he figured his own dreams would come true and the world would be his oyster.

Frost concentrated his gaze on the moors, which were engulfed in darkness. Except for a line of silhouettes that looked like a train of camel humps, there wasn't anything visible in the forbidding, black void of night.

'According to the map, it's one and a half kilometers to the building,' he announced.

Hurst said, 'Maybe she doubled back when the taxi left. Could have gone to Staithes?'

Frost glowered at him. 'Well, we'll soon

find out, won't we?'

Hurst couldn't help himself. 'We could easily miss it in the dark and we're hardly dressed for a trek. There'll be bogs out there and — '

Frost cut him off. 'It's a wonder you can get out of bed and put your feet on the floor these days, pal. But you're right, as it happens. Best we wait for first light, then go in.'

'So we spend the night in the car, do we?'

Frost shook his head, gave him his long-suffering look.

'We can hardly ask for a room at the inn. There's a place further back where we can park off the road. You'll be glad to know I put two sleeping bags in the back.'

'Bully for you,' Hurst said, not a bit enamoured.

He supposed the prospect of staying in the car was at least better than having to trudge across the moors in the dark. Hopefully, when dawn came, they'd find the woman, do what they had to and head for home.

* * *

Alex was terrified. The car was speeding along a dark lane and he didn't know who was driving, could only see a shadow in the seat next to him. Was he being kidnapped? The headlights danced crazily as the car sped around bends so fast it made his head swirl and, though he was cold, paradoxically he could feel sweat soaking his clothes. When he tried to reach across to restrain the driver, his hand hit a barrier he couldn't see or feel and he sensed that no matter how hard he pushed it would never yield, that there was nothing he could do to prevent whatever fate had in store for him. The shadow, if that's what it was, remained oblivious to his efforts.

He faced forward again as the headlights picked out a figure on the road he thought he vaguely recognized. When the car didn't slow, he tried to call out a warning but it was as though he'd lost the power of speech, his destiny to watch events evolve. The thud as the car struck vibrated through his whole body and suddenly, as though time had jumped forward, he was no longer in the car but standing on the road looking down at a body. Horrified, he realized it was Robert Walker and, even as it dawned on him, the face and body were already transforming themselves into someone else. Then he saw it was no longer Robert lying there but his own son, just as dead as the soldier had been. Crying out Jamie's name, he bent down and tried to pick him up in his arms, but that same, invisible barrier blocked him again, frustrating all his efforts and he found himself beating his fists against fresh air. His son's eyes were wide, staring at him as though expecting him to do something. He tried to dial emergency services on his mobile but no one answered and the ringing went on interminably. Why was nobody answering, for heaven's sake?

Alex woke in a sweat, a persistent ringing in his ears. It took him a moment to realize it was his bedside phone he had heard ringing. Shaking off those cruel visions of his son, he reached out, plucked the phone from the cradle and muttered his name into the mouthpiece.

The call was DI Johnson at headquarters. The Scotsman apologized for the late hour, came straight to the point.

'Bad news,' he said. 'Liz Hunt's done a runner, sometime before 10 p.m. That's when the WPC looked in the bedroom and found she'd gone. The window was open so we figure she climbed down the drainpipe.'

Alex cursed. The dream had been bad enough. Now this! It looked like he wouldn't be getting much sleep tonight.

'Thanks,' he grunted. 'I'll be right in.'

Rubbing the sleep from his eyes, he put the

phone down and dragged his body from the bed. It was on occasions like this, when his brain seemed to be fighting his body to make it move, that he sometimes wished he had a straight nine-to-five job.

Twenty minutes later he was in his office, a steaming mug of coffee in front of him as he got down to business, putting out alerts and descriptions to patrol cars and other stations across the region. He was glad that Johnson was on duty tonight because that halved the work load. His final administrative action was to allocate a young DC the task of ringing local taxi firms with Liz Hunt's description to see whether any of the drivers had spotted her.

That done, he leaned back in his chair, shut his eyes and focused on Liz Hunt. He'd come to have doubts about her and running away seemed to justify them. Now he wished he'd gone straight to the safe house, voiced his suspicion that she knew more than she was saying and seen how she'd reacted to that.

Had guilt driven her to run? Could she and her husband, or at least one of the two, have shot John Boyle out in the hills and decided, if she reported it, that would throw the police off the scent? Mitigating against that was the evidence of a chase through the woods and her shattered rear windscreen, though he supposed she or her husband could have done that themselves. Then, there was Billy Hall to consider. Had Danny Hunt shot him, or at least been involved? Alex supposed you could make it all fit if you wanted to but it was a bit like looking at an abstract painting, reading into it whatever you liked. The truth was they just hadn't enough to go on. Besides, his instincts were telling him, despite everything that might suggest otherwise, Liz Hunt seemed genuine, and he'd learned to trust his instincts.

Where was she now? It was a fair bet she'd go to her husband, though she'd claimed to have no idea of his whereabouts. Alex sighed his frustration. It was guesswork, all guesswork and only time would bring out the truth.

He hadn't bothered to switch on the main light or lower the blinds and suddenly a car's headlights swept the room, lit up his face then disappeared in an instant. It triggered an unwanted memory of his dream, which he tried to shake off, fearing it would haul him back to places he'd rather not go. But Robert Walker refused to leave, hung around in his mind like a sad ghost. He knew it was because he was wondering whether Robert's death could be linked to the recent murders, could even have been the first spark that caused them. He forced the young soldier from his thoughts. What was needed right now was more action, the most important being to find Liz Hunt and her husband.

Janet Hall, Billy's widow, came to mind. Her husband and Danny Hunt were friends so she might have an idea where Danny would go if he wanted to hide. Alex glanced at his watch. It was after midnight, late to be calling a recently bereaved widow on a long shot. After a moment's hesitation, though, he decided time was of the essence so he'd have to hope she'd understand. He reached for the phone.

'Who is this?'

Alex detected a slight irritation in the voice at the lateness of the hour.

'DI Graham, Mrs Hall,' he responded. 'I apologize for ringing this late but I've something important to ask you.'

Her tone softened. 'I was wide awake. Go ahead and ask your question.'

'Danny Hunt,' Alex said. 'We need to find him. He's off somewhere on his own and his wife doesn't know where. Do you have any idea — '

'Where he might have gone?' she interrupted.

'Do you?'

There was a silence on the other end as she thought about it.

'I'm afraid not, Inspector. Billy and Danny went to a lot of places together but I can't recall specifics. You say his wife can't help?'

Alex swallowed his disappointment. 'You know his wife, do you, Mrs Hall?'

'Not well. I only met her recently, after they were married. She seemed a pleasant girl.'

'Well, I'm sorry to have disturbed you,' Alex said. 'Can I give you my personal number in case something comes to mind?'

'Of course.'

Alex gave her his number, more in hope than expectation. He felt guilty now for disturbing her in her grief. He knew all about grief. No kind words from him could assuage it and it would run its full course. But he felt he had to say something.

'Sorry I disturbed you,' he mumbled. 'And I'm sorry about — '

'You've a job to do,' she said, cutting him off. He sensed she was afraid any words of sympathy might start her off crying on the phone. 'Don't worry, if anything comes to mind I will ring you, Inspector. You can be sure of that.'

★   ★   ★

At Liz's request the taxi drew into the lay-by not far from The Sailor Inn. She sat in the back and kept her hood up all the way just in case the police had already issued her description. Now she was ferreting in her purse for money to pay the fare, aware the driver was watching her in the mirror. He wasn't an unpleasant man but definitely the garrulous type so she'd feigned sleep most of the way.

'The inn doesn't do bed and breakfast, love,' he said. When she didn't answer him, he added, 'You must live there, do you?'

She shook her head. 'Just visiting a friend who lives in a nearby cottage.'

In the mirror she noticed his eyebrows rise, like two caterpillars synchronizing their movements.

'Don't know of any cottages around here, love. You sure?'

The question and his tone felt like a challenge, as though he were addressing an errant child.

'It's a little way onto the moors,' she said curtly, hoping he'd take the hint and stop the interrogation.

Either oblivious to it, or just plain ignoring her obvious displeasure, he continued in that same patronizing tone.

'Too dark for crossing those moors on your own. I've a daughter your age and — '

'It's not far,' she cut in. 'I know the way really well.'

She handed the money to him and opened the door.

'Be careful, now,' the driver called to her as she stepped out. The wind was cold against her cheek after the warmth of the cab but even so she was relieved to be out in the open and ready to start the last stage of the journey that would take her to her husband.

She walked into the darkness, crossed the road to the beginnings of a rough track, halted there and glanced back, hoping the inquisitive driver had gone on his way. She was annoyed to find he was still there, a bulky silhouette lit by the interior light, his stillness unsettling. Was he watching her out of curiosity or for a sinister reason? she wondered. Erring on the safe side, she walked further on until she was certain he couldn't possibly see her and waited at the side of the road. Finally, after what seemed an age, the light in the cab was extinguished and she heard the engine start up. She watched the vehicle turn around but waited until the red tail lights disappeared over the brow of a hill before she returned to the track and set off onto the moors.

The ground was rough and soaking wet in places but luckily she was wearing sturdy shoes. Twenty minutes in, she crested a rise, saw a solitary light winking in the distance and felt sure that fortune was smiling on her. The cottage was the only building in the area so it had to be the place and the light meant Danny would be inside. The terrain ahead fell away now in a steady decline which swept all the way down to the cottage and the stream that ran behind it. She pressed on, her spirit renewed because soon she would see her husband and he would end her confusion, banish those doubts she didn't want to entertain but which kept assailing her brain. Fixing her eyes on the light, the lodestar which would guide her to Danny and vindication of her faith in him, she increased her speed.

She ran the last thirty yards, banged on the wooden door, called his name. A moment later the bolt was drawn, the door creaked open and Danny was standing there holding a hurricane lamp. By its light, she could see his expression change from surprise to bemusement, finally concern.

'Liz! What the — '

He never finished the sentence because she threw her arms around his neck before he had the chance. His free arm came up, encircled her and held her tight. Neither spoke for a long time. Danny gradually released her and led her inside where she collapsed into an armchair, its springs volubly protesting their antiquity.

Danny placed the lamp on a wooden crate. She noticed the curtains looked like rags a dog had chewed and the tin roof was fighting a losing battle against rust. As she reflected on his spartan existence here, he turned to face her, that haunted look in his eyes, the one she hadn't seen for a long time and dreaded, reminding her of days she'd hoped had gone forever.

'Why on earth have you come here in the dark, Liz?' he asked. 'It's far too dangerous out there at night. I can hardly believe . . . '

She couldn't help her tears, hated herself for giving in to her emotions. Danny knew she didn't cry easily and seeing her like that would really worry him. He didn't say anything, just sat on the arm of the chair, put his hand on her shoulder and dug his fingers into her flesh like a grappling iron binding her to him. That physical contact was his way of letting her know that, whatever was troubling her, he was there for her and it had the desired effect. She dried her tears, wishing they could stay like that, hold the moment.

'Tell me,' he said, eventually.

He listened without interrupting as she told him everything. Tears came into his eyes when he learned his friends had been

146

murdered. When she'd finished, except for those tears coursing down his cheeks, he was so still and quiet it was as though he'd turned to stone

In the silence, Liz was conscious of the wind rattling the roof as it searched for a way into their little world. By the flickering light of the hurricane lamp, she noticed the hollows in his cheeks, the outline of bone under the skin and worried he was starting to waste away as he had when the traumas of Afghanistan had eaten at him like a parasitic worm.

'My God,' he suddenly burst out, 'you could have been killed. I could have lost you.'

His voice seemed to come from faraway, a place where he'd been trying to come to terms with what she'd told him and was failing. 'Like Billy and John,' he added plaintively.

She was bursting to ask him questions but reined herself in. If he knew anything, she wanted him to share it willingly rather than having to be pressed for it.

Now she felt his body tense and his shoulders started to heave as though he was shaking with suppressed laughter. She knew the signs and pulled him close while over and over again he apologized for breaking down. She told him it was nothing to be ashamed of, wondered if the cause was old wounds re-opening or fresh troubles plaguing his soul, reversing the progress he'd made.

The shaking didn't last. When it subsided he drew away from her and their eyes locked. She thought he was ready now, that he would tell her and she would understand and they would face whatever it was together. But when he opened his mouth words seemed to fail him. Guiltily, he slid his eyes away, focused on the lamp as though if he stared hard enough he could lose himself in the flame and free his mind of its troubles. Liz could wait no longer.

'Do you know why your pals were murdered, Danny?'

Like a moth drawn to light, he continued to stare at the lamp. Why wouldn't he answer? Could it be for her sake? she wondered. Whatever his reason, he was testing her patience to the limits now.

'I told the police lies, Danny,' she said, trying to hide her exasperation. 'I did that because I was being true to you. I'm your wife and I believe in you. So tell me.'

His head swivelled in her direction and his shoulders slumped forward as though he was burdened with an invisible weight too heavy to bear.

'Blackmail,' he mumbled.

'Who was being blackmailed? Was it you?'

He shook his head. 'Not me. Billy and John were blackmailing . . . someone. I wouldn't go along with them.'

Those two were his friends, more than friends, nearer to brothers; good, honest men, according to her husband and she trusted his judgment. What was he saying?

'You mean you wouldn't join them in their plan?'

His eyes had been dull. Now they blazed and she knew he was disappointed she'd needed to ask.

'You know me better, don't you?'

The reprimand gutted her. She felt herself blush and reached for his hand. Her mouth was suddenly dry.

'I'm stressed out, Danny. You need to tell me everything and then maybe I'll feel better.'

He squeezed her hand. 'You've been through it, haven't you. I'm so sorry.'

That was the man she knew talking and she waited thinking he understood and would soon enlighten her. But he remained stubbornly silent.

'Danny!'

An uncomfortable atmosphere developed, became an oppressive presence in the room. Somewhere out there in the night an owl screeched. Liz shivered involuntarily. The noise reminded her that there were men after her, that outside there was a world where hunters roamed, eyes alert for an opportunity to punish a careless move.

Danny put his face in his hands, his fingers forming bars over his eyes. He spoke in a melancholy monotone.

'They said it would be easy money but I wouldn't agree to it. I argued, pleaded with them not to do it, but it was no use. I thought about going to the police but they were ... like brothers.' He paused a moment and when he spoke again it was with sneering self-contempt.

'I came here to think things out, or so I told myself. Really I was just running away, avoiding the responsibility. Should have gone to the police. Now they're dead because of me.' His face grew dark. 'He must have hired those killers.'

Another noise intruded, this time a soft, rhythmic flutter of wings. A moment later it was followed by a screech so faint it was barely audible, yet unmistakably one of pain.

'I know they were close to you,' Liz said. 'It's understandable you needed time to think. But why go to all this length? Why didn't you tell me, Danny?'

'Wanted to keep you out of it,' he mumbled, not meeting her eye. 'If you didn't

150

know, you couldn't be blamed ... for anything.'

She could just about see his logic. He'd always been protective but she was a full-grown woman and he should have shared his problem with her. Still, he hadn't committed a crime. And yet she felt that there was something he was holding back.

'Who did they want to blackmail, Danny? What did they know about someone that was so bad?'

Her husband thrust out his jaw, a mannerism she knew meant he'd made up his mind about something and wouldn't be moved.

'Can't tell you that.'

Danny hiding something important from her didn't seem natural; it was an aberration in his nature.

'Why not? After all I've been through I think I have a right to know, don't you?'

'Forget about it,' he said, an eyebrow twitching nervously.

Liz's temper started to rise. This wasn't fair. Danny had been a soldier. In the same way a soldier would want to know why he was going into a war zone to risk his life, she needed to know why she was in danger. Surely he could see that.

'You'll have to go to the police,' she said,

curtly. 'Tell them what you can't tell me.'

'I'd already decided to do that but it's too late now.'

Liz sighed her exasperation. 'Look, the truth will come out. Better I learn it from you.'

'Leave it, woman!' he snapped.

His voice had such unexpected power that she recoiled. Even at his worst, after Afghanistan, he had never been so aggressive towards her.

His tone much quieter, he said, 'Look, let me think about it. Maybe I'll tell you tomorrow when you're rested. Got to decide what's best.'

She was disappointed but at least he was thinking about it and she reckoned she could wait until morning. Her consolation was that she'd heard from her husband's own lips that he wasn't involved with his friends' misdeeds and her faith had been justified. The fact that those killers could have no reason to be hunting him was a relief, too.

Danny pointed to the single bed.

'You take the bed and the sleeping bag. I'll be okay in the chair.'

Without a word, she rose, went over to the bed. When she zipped up the sleeping bag, Danny stood over her, a vague look in his eyes.

'I loved my friends,' he said, his voice just audible. 'They looked out for me and I looked out for them. We went through hell together. They weren't bad men . . . didn't deserve . . . '

Liz knew that he was trying to excuse his bad temper towards her a moment earlier.

'I understand.'

'Afghanistan!' He spoke the word like a curse. 'It damaged them. They were broken men. If I hadn't had you maybe I'd have gone down that road. Without you . . . '

He paused, lost for words. She noticed he was tense, his eyes wide, as though he'd caught a glimpse of hell and feared he would soon be dragged down into its depths. Liz worried that all the progress he'd made would erode and he'd be back where he'd been before.

'We'll get through this,' she told him, 'by sticking together like always.'

'I love you,' he muttered then turned off the lamp, retreated to the chair, lowered himself into it and pulled a blanket over his body.

Though she was tired, Liz didn't doze off because now that she was still the consequences of her actions were starting to hit home and trouble her. The police would no doubt be looking for her, would think she had something to hide, perhaps information about the murders, or worse, personal involvement in the crimes. None of that was true, of course, but it could look that way, so the quicker she and Danny went to the police and straightened things out the better. The only trouble was that her husband had been reluctant to tell her everything and, as she drifted off to sleep, that niggled away because it wasn't like him to hide things from her.

* * *

Frost lay awake in the car, enjoying the dark nothingness beyond the windscreen. When he was a kid, after one of those beatings administered by his drunken stepfather, he'd retreat to the sanctuary of his bedroom, lie down with the curtains open staring out at the blackness. It had been a source of comfort because it had meant respite from that bully and the erratic mood swings of his alcoholic mother. The darkness, which held terrors for many a little one, was more like a friend whose embrace he welcomed because, though devoid of human warmth, it was neutral, would never let him down.

Hurst stirred in the passenger seat, let out a curse.

'Can't sleep,' he groaned. 'This is the last

time in my life I'll ever sleep in a car, so help me.'

Frost smirked. 'The question is will you ever sleep with that wife of yours again.'

'Bit below the belt that one, Frosty, even for you,' Hurst grunted.

'Well, you reckon she's playing away, don't you? Can't wait to catch her at it, you said.'

'Too right, mate, and when I do I'll dispose of the cuckoo who's been in my nest. Then, I'll be living the high life while she's on the social and shopping in Pound Stretchers.'

'Generous of you to let her live. You're all heart, mate.'

Hurst grunted. 'She's got my son to look after, hasn't she? Ain't so much of a bastard as to deprive my son of a mother when I've flown. Anyway, what about you? Going to finish tarting up stiffs for the last journey on coffin road, are you?'

'Very witty for you, Hurst. The answer is I enjoy it, especially the embalming. It's an art form, like being a sculptor. You wouldn't understand the aestheticism involved, a philistine like you.'

'Kind of defeats the purpose, though, getting a corpse all prettied up like he's going to a dance or something.'

'Last thing you can do for a mortal soul, mate. Matter of respect for the dead and their

155

nearest and dearest.' He grinned wolfishly. 'Never know, might have to do it for you one day, but don't worry about it. I'll make sure your shoes are polished so you can see your face in them and that untidy mop of yours is combed for once.'

Hurst gave a shiver. Even after all these years he still didn't understand Frost. One thing was for sure, though, he didn't intend dying before him, so there was no chance he'd be mucking about with his body.

'Do you think you're a psychopath, Frosty?' he asked, eventually. 'No, let me re-phrase that . . . are you and me psychopaths?'

'Define a psychopath.'

'Can't! That's why I'm asking. Just a word I heard someone apply to stone-cold killers. Seen that film *Psycho* as well, but I ain't weird like that feller, dressing up as his mother and all.'

'Well, let's see now . . . ' Frost considered for a moment. 'Do you . . . did you ever . . . love that wife of yours?'

Hurst screwed his face up, thought hard.

'Suppose so. I married her, didn't I?'

Frost smiled to himself. He thought about asking his partner to define love but considered that would be expecting too much. He figured love was mainly a delusion anyway. People just used each other and moved on, had done since time immemorial no matter how they sugar-coated it. Hurst surely had to look no further than his wife to realize that.

'Let me put it another way,' he mused. 'All these years have you just pretended to be my friend?'

Frost figured he knew the answer already, that probably even back in their service days their partnership had been one of mutual convenience rather than any deep bonding. For sure, that's how it was nowadays and he was well aware Hurst didn't like the way he was the dominant one who gave the orders.

'Of course not!'

'Don't worry, then.' Frost smiled at his partner's straight-faced lie. 'You're not a psychopath because you have feelings.'

Hurst exhaled. He was no further forward in regard to his question because he didn't consider his partner a friend, only kept up the pretence that he did.

'Don't like that word 'psychopath'. It sounds like it means mad. Thought maybe all killers like us were psychopaths.'

Frost found it hard not to laugh. Was Hurst, like most near retirees, looking back and wondering what quirk of fate had led him down his particular path in life rather than so many others he might have followed? His next question seemed to confirm that hypothesis.

'Ever wonder how we ended up in this game?'

'Broke the taboo, mate.'

'Taboo? What's a taboo?'

Frost sighed. 'You ask more questions than a kid. Something strictly forbidden, that's a taboo, see? Way back it was decided a human life was a sacred thing and so killing another person was forbidden. Those guys who take a life break the taboo.'

'Doesn't apply in war, though, eh? Our first kills were in Iraq. Rag-heads don't count.'

Frost yawned. He was getting bored.

'Dead right . . . if you'll pardon the pun. The thing is, once you've done it, broken the taboo, you realize how easy it is, how there's no supernatural consequence, no punishment, no lightning going to strike you down.' He paused. 'Just for a moment, you're a god of destruction, feel your own power. No greater feeling than that, if you ask me.'

He could sense Hurst's eyes on him in the dark, wondered what he was thinking. It was the first time in all these years the subject had come up.

'That's too complicated for me,' Hurst said eventually.

'Thought it might be.'

'When I pull the trigger, I just think of the money and that's all.'

'Just be pleased you're not a psychopath, then,' Frost told him, amused at the irony.

Hurst laughed. 'That's what I'll tell my wife after I've killed the boyfriend. It'll make me feel better.'

'That's in the future,' Frost said. 'Right now you should get some sleep. That bitch gave us the slip in those woods, remember. When the sun rises we'll need to be switched on.'

★ ★ ★

The change in his wife's breathing told Danny she was asleep and he lay there wondering whether he'd done the right thing. He'd felt guilty going off and leaving her but much more so when he'd heard what had happened in his absence. Those of a religious turn of mind might, he supposed, have called it karma, or God's punishment for thinking he could avoid consequences. All he knew was that he'd made a mess of things because he'd been reluctant to betray his friends, to bring pain into Liz's life. The truth will come out in the end, Liz had told him. All he'd really done was delay it with his foolish actions and in the process put her in danger.

He rose from the armchair, rooted around in his rucksack for his binoculars, soft padded it to the window, opened the curtains and settled down on a straight-backed chair. The moon gave him about fifty yards' visibility but he figured his field of vision would extend to double that once his eyes adjusted. Not wanting to scare his wife, he'd avoided talking about the men who were after her. But those killers were on his mind. Liz seemed convinced she was safe but from what she'd told him he thought it was more than possible they would still be looking for her. He was sure they were hired professionals and men like that didn't give up easily, had ways and means of finding their quarry. In Afghanistan, carelessness cost lives and he'd learned the value of staying alert, even when it seemed there was no immediate threat. If those men did come, he wanted an advantage, however slight, because it could make all the difference.

An hour later he noticed a meteor shower shooting across the sky. It reminded him of tracer bullets chasing each other in the dark and triggered those old memories he was trying to bury. In spite of his efforts to drive them off, they persisted. In his mind he heard rifle fire, voices shouting urgent commands and remembered that sense of death in the air, each man in his section hoping it wouldn't come for him but only too aware of his vulnerability. That familiar hollowness crept into the pit of his stomach, nihilistic thoughts into his brain. He breathed in deeply, started to count, tactics he'd learned in order to distract himself when the moods came. This time the demons retreated but left behind a different fear, the fear that, if he was tested again, he wouldn't cope, because he'd seen the cruelty in men's hearts and didn't want to discover it in his own.

★　★　★

Liz felt something touch her shoulder, opened her eyes and gave a start. The momentary panic left her when she realized it was Danny standing over her and remembered she was safe in the cottage. She figured it must be early morning because thin shafts of light were slanting through gaps in the curtains like probing fingers encroaching on their sanctuary from the world outside. As sleep fell away, she noticed the binoculars hanging around her husband's neck and, when she looked closer at his face, the anxious set of his jaw.

'Come to the window,' he commanded, his tone leaving no room for doubt it was urgent.

By the time she rose, Danny was already back at the window. Like a hunter in a hide, his whole being seemed to be concentrated on whatever he could see out on the moors. She stood beside him, followed his gaze, could see nothing but empty moorland.

'Up there,' he told her, 'on the ridge.'

The sun was rising behind the ridge, subjugating what remained of the dark to its all-conquering will. Two figures were silhouetted at the highest point. She thought initially it was foxes out hunting, but even as the idea entered her head, she knew it couldn't be accurate because the figures were too upright.

'Men,' she said, closing her eyes and sucking in a deep breath.

Danny nodded, handed her the binos. 'The light's improving all the time. See if you can make them out.'

The figures suddenly stopped moving. As she focused the binos a silent scream reverberated in her head. Her legs threatened to give way. How could she ever forget those faces, those cruel features burned on her brain? She turned to Danny, reluctant to say it but she didn't have to because Danny interpreted the desperate fear in her eyes.

'It's them, isn't it? The men who are after you?'

She found it hard to speak, nodded affirmation.

After a moment's silence, she said, 'What are we to do, Danny?'

He didn't answer and their eyes returned to the ridge. Already it seemed lighter, the sun stretching itself lazily into all the nooks and crannies, illuminating the expanse of yellow gorse, pock-marked by purple bracken, which Liz had crossed in the dark last night on her way down here. She thought the cottage must stand out like a lone tree in vast swathes of grassland. Her lip quivering, she turned away from the window.

'We're trapped in here,' she groaned. 'We'll have to run for it and take our chances on the moors.'

Danny shook his head 'No good. They'll see us and they'll be too fast for us.'

Before she could think, he grasped her arm, pulled her across the room and out the back door. Only yards away, she could hear the stream gurgling like a baby, a sound so soothing it was incongruous with her sense of desperation. Danny pointed across flat moorland to an isolated copse which stood like a lone fortress a quarter mile beyond the stream. Beyond that, the land was flat all the way to the horizon.

'The road is not far beyond the copse,'

Danny said. 'If we can get to the copse unseen, we might have a chance of making it to the road and we can stop a car.'

Liz just wanted to get as far away as possible from those men and considered any action was better than waiting for them to arrive at the cottage. Keen to get on with it, she took a step forward and Danny had to haul her back again.

'They're higher than us, which means they'll see us soon as we move out.' He pointed to a water butt adjoining the wall. 'We'll use that to get on this side of the roof where we won't be visible. As soon as they're inside the cottage we'll run for it.'

Liz bit her lip. The plan made sense but was far from perfect. What if they didn't go straight inside but circled the cottage first?

'We might not get enough of a start,' she ventured.

'We'll head for the stream. The banks will give us cover to work our way level with the copse. It'll cut down the distance where we're exposed to about two hundred yards. After that . . . ' Danny didn't need to spell out the rest and his voice trailed away.

She followed him back inside, watched him gather up two waterproof smocks, one green, the other army camouflage. He threw the camouflage one to her, put the other one on himself, then he picked up a hunting knife, which lay on the table, sheathed it on his belt and hurried back to the window. Liz reluctantly joined him there.

Danny's body stiffened like a dog preparing for a fight. Liz followed his gaze and let out a gasp. The men were only a hundred yards away from the cottage. She hadn't expected them to move so fast. The gorse had restricted her own speed last night but it didn't seem an impediment to them because they were moving effortlessly. Both were wearing black anoraks, which reminded her of those black tracksuits they'd worn in the woods . . . executioners' colours. She could feel her heart thumping in her chest. This was all her fault. They must have followed her here and her actions had put Danny in danger. She didn't have time to dwell on it, though, because Danny grabbed her hand, pulled her to the back door and ushered her outside.

Danny shut the door behind them, climbed onto the water butt and helped her up beside him. Using the gutter, he hauled himself up onto the roof and reached down for her. She grasped his hand, feet scrambling against the wall for purchase, climbed up and lay down beside him, already breathing hard. When she glanced up, she could see the clouds scudding across the sky like puffs of smoke exhaled from a giant's mouth and suddenly she felt insignificant and vulnerable, her fate depending on luck and chance as much as on her own actions.

★ ★ ★

Alex forced one eye open, stared at the luminous clock face, saw it was 4 a.m. and groaned. The phone had woken him but at least he hadn't been in the middle of a nightmare. As he picked up, he feared whoever was ringing at this time must be the bearer of bad news.

'Inspector Graham? Is that you?'

The voice belonged to a woman but was so quiet and hesitant at first he didn't recognize it.

'Who is this, please?' he asked, blinking sleep out of his eyes.

'It's Janet Hall, Inspector. Sorry to disturb you at this hour but you did say . . . '

He remembered why he'd given the widow his home number and tried to concentrate his thoughts, wondered whether she'd recalled something that might help them find Danny Hunt.

'Don't worry about it,' he told her. 'I told you to call anytime.'

'I couldn't sleep, Inspector, so I started to look through old photographs, post cards, reminders of . . . '

He heard the sob in her voice, imagined her wiping away tears. Widowhood was a cruel thing, as bad as losing a son, and he wanted to sympathize but settled instead for patience. It took her a moment to compose herself. Then she told him.

'I came across a postcard sent many years ago, around the time we were courting. It was from Danny Hunt to Billy. Maybe it could help you.'

'What is it that makes you think that, Janet?'

'There's a picture on one side of the postcard of The Sailor Inn. It's near Staithes. On the other side of the card there's just one word written, 'cottage', with six numbers after it. It's signed 'Danny'.'

'The numbers could be a grid reference,' Alex mused, wondering whether any of this could be relevant, given the passage of time.

'More than likely,' the widow said. 'I do remember Billy telling me when they were young they used to go off onto the moors together. Danny had a relative who owned a cottage. I think they stayed there.'

'You've done well,' Alex told her, 'and I will follow it up. Give me those numbers and try to get some rest now, won't you?'

'Inspector, I need to know.' Her voice had suddenly become much more powerful and he thought he could detect a vicious undertone. 'Could what I've told you help find Billy's killer?'

'I'm not sure. Perhaps it will. Rest assured I'll keep you posted.'

She let out a mournful sigh. 'Well, I hope it does. I hope you find him and do to him what he did to Billy.'

Alex understood well enough her desire for revenge. He'd drunk deep from that poisoned well himself, the devil's brew. Sometimes he could still taste it, didn't think it would ever go away entirely. Did it ever leave those robbed of their loved ones by another human? Since Jamie's death, he thought he'd become more understanding of other people's troubles and tragedies, in that regard was a better person, he supposed, but alone in bed at night, with his melancholy memories of his son keeping him awake, that was about as comforting as wearing nothing but a string vest in an Arctic storm.

'I promise you no stone will be left unturned,' he said solemnly. 'Now, can you just give me those numbers?'

★ ★ ★

Liz and Danny lay on the roof as exposed and helpless as two turtles stranded on a beach waiting for the tide to come in, their fear married to terrible anticipation. Each second felt like an eternity now and their nerves were as taut as elastic drawn to breaking point. Liz could feel Danny's hard, tensed muscles against her body. Would it be the last sensation she would ever feel? Was there even a chance her husband's hurriedly conceived strategy could work? It was hard to believe that they could outrun those killers; she'd already had a terrible foretaste of that, had only managed to escape by the skin of her teeth.

In the forbidding landscape beyond the stream, a movement distracted her and she saw a fox lope into view. She watched as it halted and stood perfectly still, its sharp face turned in her direction. Then, as though a cunning prescience warned it that other predators were homing in on its territory intent on killing, it turned and dashed into the bracken. The fox's elusiveness was in such stark contrast to her own frozen inertia; she felt a pang of jealousy for the animal.

The sound made by the front door crashing felt like an uncouth insult to the peace and silence of the moors and a shockwave passed through her body while, beside her, Danny

169

tensed and dug his fingers into her arm. Then their eyes met in unspoken confirmation that it was time to run.

Danny didn't hesitate, slid down the roof onto the water butt, held his arms in the air like a priest beseeching the heavens and helped her down. Soon as they hit the ground, they started running. Liz, conscious that at any moment those men might emerge from the back door and shoot them down, felt the hairs on the back of her neck bristle. In front of them, the stream murmured encouragement and, reaching it, they slid down the grassy bank on their backsides, finished up in the stream with water up to their knees.

They'd only just made it because soon the back door crashed open and they heard the men's voices. Danny started moving, leading the way along the stream bed, using rocks in the shallows for footholds. Liz mirrored his movements, followed each twist and turn until he called a halt. When he scrambled up the bank, she followed behind and lay beside him in the grass. Together, they looked back at the cottage.

The men were outside the building fifty yards from their position but it seemed no distance at all. Liz estimated it was around four hundred yards to the copse. If they made a break for it, they were sure to be spotted.

Their only hope was that the men would go back inside, or head off in another direction. That hope soon ended, when one of the men pointed to the ground near the water butt. Danny cursed and told Liz the men had discovered their footprints.

The killers started off towards the stream. With the wind billowing their anoraks they looked like two birds of ill omen, black wings flapping, the stench of death upon them. Just for a moment, it felt like a film shoot rather than real life because this kind of thing didn't happen in real life, not to people like her and her husband. But she knew well enough that no director was about to shout cut and end her misery.

She glanced at her husband. His eyes were fixed on the men. She knew he was trying to figure a way out for them but thought it nigh on impossible that he would come up with one now. If they made a move, any move, a bullet in the back of the head would soon dispatch them to the afterlife. She felt like giving up, surrendering to the inevitable. Why drag out this terror? The feeling soon passed, though, because she wanted desperately to live and, crazy as it sounded, bring those wanton killers to justice.

Danny suddenly scrambled back down the bank, ferreted around in the shallower part of the stream. He scooped up a handful of stones, selected two, discarded the others and came back to her.

'Used to be good at aiming grenades,' he said, breathlessly. 'Going to try something. I'll aim for the cottage and hope the noise will distract them. That'll be our chance to make a break for the copse. Get ready to run.'

Before she had a chance to answer, he positioned himself in the middle of the stream, drew back his arm and launched the first stone. She lost sight of it but saw it hadn't disturbed the killers. Praying he'd be accurate, she followed the second stone's trajectory. It bounced off the tin roof with a noise like a rifle shot. The killers heard it this time and spun round, stared at each other for a moment, then sprinted back to the cottage and disappeared inside.

'It worked,' she told Danny. 'Get going!'

They ran up the far bank onto the open moor. Aware every yard and every second counted, Liz cursed the thick patches of bracken that seemed alive with hands trying to clutch at her legs and slow her down. She didn't waste time or energy looking behind, focused all her attention on the copse like a runner on the finishing line, the landscape merely a blur. At last they reached the trees. As they burst through a crow took flight, the fluttering of its wings frightening her for a moment, making her heart thump harder. Daring to hope, she turned, looked back over the moor. Her hope soon drained away like water through a sieve, leaving her with nothing but despair. Danny's body visibly sagged. The men had crossed the stream, were coming fast, and the copse, which they'd hoped would be their sanctuary, had turned into a trap.

★　★　★

Alex was surprised his map reading skills weren't as rusty as he'd imagined. He'd crested a ridge and there it was, the cottage Janet Hall had told him about. He supposed he could have charged someone else with the task of checking it out but had decided to do it himself. He knew that he might not find the Hunts down there and this might be a wasted trip, but at least he'd enjoyed the walk and it was worth it just to see the early morning sun painting the moors, light and shadow chasing each other.

He found the door wide open and when he called out there was no reply. Crossing the threshold, the first thing he noticed was that the back door was wide open and he thought it strange the place should be left so exposed to the elements. Then he saw blankets on the bed, a fresh loaf and butter on a rough table. A rucksack lay open on the floor, its contents strewn around as though someone had rummaged through it in a hurry. Obviously someone had been here and very recently, too.

He exited the back door, let his eyes drift over the landscape. The only sign of movement was a glimpse of a fox loping across the bracken, its head turned in his direction. Back inside again, he found a grey parka behind the door and remembered Liz Hunt had reportedly worn one like that when she'd run from the safe house. All the signs pointed to something not quite right. Someone had left in a big hurry. Had the occupants seen him on the ridge and fled? he wondered. He carried on searching, hoping to find some clue to confirm his suspicions that Liz Hunt had definitely been there. When, more in hope than expectation, he looked under the mattress, he found a brown envelope. He opened it, withdrew the photograph he found inside and, hardly believing the evidence of his own eyes, stared at it in disbelief.

It had been taken in a street at night but he could still recognize Billy Hall and John Boyle standing next to each other and figured it must belong to Danny Hunt. He looked closer, noticed another person in the background, a male whose features he couldn't quite make out leaning on a car partially hidden in an alley. Someone had drawn an arrow pointing at his head. What significance did the photograph have for Liz Hunt's husband? he wondered. Why had he felt the need to hide it under the mattress?

Now that Alex knew for certain Danny had been here, two possibilities struck him. Maybe husband and wife had seen him coming down from the ridge and had fled in a hurry or, in a much worse scenario he didn't like to dwell on, those assassins had followed Liz here, caught the couple inside, killed them and hidden the bodies out there on the moor. That fox he'd seen had perhaps been drawn to the area by the scent of blood. But he knew he was making assumptions and, anyway, there was little he would be able to accomplish alone. A search team and helicopter were needed so, not wanting to waste valuable time, with a long, regretful sigh, he used his mobile to ring headquarters and make the arrangements. Then, aiming to meet the team back on the main road, he began to retrace his route in.

★ ★ ★

175

Liz read it in her husband's face. He wouldn't tell her but she already knew that there wasn't much hope. If they left the copse, tried to make it to the main road, they were certain to be caught in the open, gunned down like a couple of grouse in the hunting season. In possession of a gun, they might have had a chance, but their only weapon was Danny's hunting knife. Uttering a silent prayer, she instinctively looked to the heavens, gave a start when she noticed a crow staring down at her from a branch, its eyes as black as its wings. As though it sensed she was watching it, the crow performed a nifty little dance and cawed. In the same instant, his friends and neighbours took up the refrain, their corvine cacophony echoing through the woods. It spooked Liz, pushing her nerves even nearer the edge. It was too much like mockery, as though the birds were revelling in the fact that this time they weren't the ones being hunted and were looking forward to the spectacle.

Danny grabbed her hand, dragged her after him, deeper into the copse. It was like reliving that other terrible chase all over again, the only difference being that this time her husband was with her. Every sound was amplified: their ragged breathing; the swish of branches resisting the wind as it wormed its way through the canopy above them; the rustle of dead leaves underfoot.

Danny halted and she bumped against him. His eyes darted everywhere and behind them she could see his mind working furiously, choices that could lead to life or death colliding in his brain. She noticed he was gripping the hilt of his knife so hard his knuckles were like white snow peaks.

'We've got to hide,' he muttered eventually, but his voice lacked the strength of conviction.

She followed him further into the copse, into waist-high bracken where he told her to lie down and, working like a man possessed, spread fallen leaves over her body. She didn't protest because she knew there was no time for argument and she had to trust her husband.

A fallen tree lay only yards away, a sad giant cut down in its prime. Danny scrambled under it, burrowed into the small space like a wild animal going to ground in desperation when the hunt is closing in. He lay still and she could only see his face.

Liz was terrified, didn't dare move. Those men were trackers so how long could they hide here? More than ever before, she realized the fragility of a human life, the paper-thin divide between survival and extinction. Were they destined to die here, she and Danny? Would their bodies be eaten by animals and insects until all that remained as evidence they'd ever existed were vestigial bones? A branch snapped, bruising the silence. It was followed by a muffled sound, indistinct at first, then recognizable as a man's voice. Liz cowered down lower.

For what seemed an eternity, nothing stirred. Even the birds were quiet. She thought maybe the killers had passed by, that maybe they'd be lucky, would be able to hide until dark, sneak away then. That hope disintegrated a moment after its conception when, like a ghost manifesting out of thin air, one of the men loomed into view beyond the fallen tree. The lower part of his body was hidden by the trunk so that he appeared to be floating rather than walking. Danny wouldn't be able to see him from where he lay. She desperately wanted to warn him of the danger but didn't dare risk moving a muscle.

The man stopped a few yards from her husband's hiding place. Liz hoped it was only her imagination that made her think he was looking straight at her. Heart beating faster, she pressed her face hard against the ground hoping, if Danny saw her do that, he'd know one of the men was near.

She counted silently until she thought a

minute had passed, then couldn't resist raising her head a fraction and squinting out of one eye. Now the killer was standing with one leg on top of the log, holding his gun across his chest, so calm it was as though he was on a nature ramble. Danny wouldn't be aware of his proximity and she was afraid the killer would clamber over the tree trunk, shoot her husband before he could even scramble out of his lair. Her fear of that happening soared when, a moment later, he stepped up onto the log, a mere two feet above Danny's position, then dropped onto the ground so that his feet were less than a yard from Danny's face. Liz willed him not to turn but a primitive sixth sense seemed to warn him and he spun around, saw Danny's head and pointed the gun straight at her husband.

'Come out, come out, wherever you are,' he sang, like a child playing hide and seek.

Danny didn't respond, but he was trapped and there was nothing he could do about it. Any movement he made to resist would be restricted, telegraphed to the man with the gun in plenty of time to counter it.

'Okay! Suit yourself, then,' the man said in a sing-song voice. 'I'll kill you there. Just tell me where the bitch is hiding first.'

Liz had heard enough. Blood pounding against her temples like drumsticks, she rose out of the bracken and sprinted across the intervening ground. He heard her coming, turned, but was too late. With all the instinct of a she-cat defending her own, she aimed for his face with her nails and drew blood. The sudden ferocity of her attack made him recoil but, once the element of surprise was gone, he hurled her off just as she tried to sink her teeth into his jugular.

She hit the ground hard, the pain of the impact vibrating through her whole body. Twisting onto her back, she tried to rise again but something pressing hard against her temple prevented her. She knew it was the barrel of the gun and that her effort had been in vain. Looking up, she saw an angry face staring at her and she knew she would receive no mercy from this man. As she waited in a state of acceptance for the bullet that would end it, her only regret was that she and Danny were being robbed of their future.

'Die, bitch!'

She closed her eyes, began to pray but, as she asked forgiveness for her sins, she realized the barrel was no longer pressing against her temple. She thought the killer must be toying with her, drawing out her suffering for his own sadistic satisfaction and reluctantly opened her eyes, expecting the reprieve to be brief.

It took her a moment to digest the scene before her. Danny was standing a yard away with his back to her supporting the killer, whose head was drooping over his shoulder. There was no anger in the killer's face now, only a look of disbelief, the face of a child who's just been told there's no Santa Claus. When Danny lowered him to the ground she saw the hunting knife protruding from his stomach and blood suffusing from the wound, black as treacle on his parka. Her husband was looking at his hands as though he couldn't believe what he had done and Liz hoped he wasn't drifting off into that world of his own where it was hard to reach him; the other killer wouldn't be far away and he couldn't afford to break down now.

'Didn't want to do it,' he muttered. 'Had enough . . . '

'You had to,' Liz told him, gripping his arm. 'It was him or us and it's not over yet. You're the soldier here. I'm depending on you!'

It seemed to do the trick. His face became animated again and she knew he was back with her, that he was going to be all right, that he'd stepped back from the abyss. He grabbed her hand and they set off running again until they reached the far side of the copse where they halted, stared back into the trees. Nothing was stirring behind them and ahead, way in the distance, they could see the thin ribbon of road. It represented salvation, but the open ground had to be crossed and, if the other killer caught them out there on the moors, it would be easy for him to gun them down. A gunshot exploded in the trees behind them and, though too far away to have been aimed at them, it was a potent reminder that a decision couldn't be delayed. Liz just wanted to run but Danny had other ideas.

'Give me your anorak and jumper!'

He was already removing his own anorak and sounded so decisive she did as she was told, grateful he seemed to be back in command of himself and able to take the initiative.

★　★　★

Hurst called his partner's name without receiving an answer. He figured he must either be so close to their quarry he couldn't reply, or he was dead, which didn't seem at all likely.

When he thought he saw a movement straight ahead, he instantly went into a crouch and started to circle, hoping it was the fugitives so he could end this farce now.

Closer to the spot, he realized it was Frost lying against a fallen tree trunk, could hardly believe his eyes when he saw the hunting knife sticking out of his gut. Amazed that two amateurs had got the better of him, he approached cautiously and knelt down. Frost had his eyes shut, but sensing his presence, opened them.

'It's bad . . . ' he groaned.

'Can see that, matey.'

'So get moving and dress the wound, then help me get out of here,' Frost said, grimacing in pain. 'The road isn't far. There's a chance . . . with your help.'

Hurst couldn't help admiring his cheek. Even hurt badly, he was still giving out with the orders, talking like a superior to a subordinate. In a way, Hurst found it satisfying that he was in character because his attitude would add savour to the surprise he had in store for him!

'Big mistake, Frost.'

Frost stared at him, uncomprehending, winced as a spasm of pain hit him.

'No time to waffle,' he gasped. 'Just get me out of here!'

Hurst grinned. It felt good to be in control, no longer the subservient one. This wasn't exactly how he had been planning things, long term. But, hey. Needs must!

'My wife will miss you,' he said. 'But I won't. Got sick of you a long time ago.'

Frost's mouth opened wide, stayed that way as his brain worked out that his partner knew, must have known for a while now. Hurst could see in his eyes he'd got the message. After waiting so long for this moment, he was determined to rub it in, extract maximum satisfaction.

'That's right. You both took me for a fool but I knew you were messing about behind my back.'

Frost's shoulders visibly sagged. He stared vacantly into space, like a defeated boxer on the canvas who knows, no matter how much his brain tells him to get up, it would be to no avail because the fight is over and he can't win.

'Enjoyed playing you both,' Hurst chirruped. 'I was going to take you out at one of your little trysts. Won't have that satisfaction now, will I?' He paused, assumed what he thought was a reflective air. 'Still, you can't have everything and all the money will compensate.'

When he finished speaking, he reached forward, gave a histrionic flourish with his wrist, gripped the knife and twisted. Frost let out a guttural cry of pain that echoed though the copse and was mimicked by the watching crows.

'Payback time, mate!' Hurst grunted. 'But at least the knife is in the front. Better than the one in the back you gave me, don't you think?'

'Damn you,' Frost screeched. 'Get it over with!'

Hurst cocked his head to one side pretending offence, then pointed the gun.

'It gives me great satisfaction,' he said, teeth clenched, 'to dissolve our partnership.'

The bullet smacked into the centre of Frost's forehead. His head jerked back hard against the tree trunk. Blood started to pour out of the bullet hole and run down his face like little red worms wriggling their way to freedom. His dead eyes gazed out vacantly at the world he'd left behind but didn't disconcert Hurst in the slightest. He'd seen that look so many times in the past he'd lost any sense of wonderment or curiosity about the moment a life ended. All he felt was satisfaction that Frost had paid the price for betraying him.

He didn't linger because there was still a job to finish. Studying the ground, it only took seconds to pick up the fugitives' tracks and start on their trail. The signs were blatant enough and as he followed them it amused him to think Frost, who had taken such pride preparing dead bodies for burial in his day job, would have hated the idea of his body being left to rot on the forest floor.

★　★　★

Finding Frost stuck like a pig had surprised Hurst. He didn't want to die like that in this miserable place, let that excuse for a wife have all his hard-earned money. Frost had spoken about the Hunt woman with respect. Was she the one who'd done for him? Or the guy with her? Whatever, they were amateurs, out of their depth and it should never have happened. Frost must have been dreaming about running off with his wife, dropped his guard for once.

For a man who'd trained in the jungles of Belize, it was like following in the wake of two rampaging elephants. It soon became evident to him that they were heading to the far side of the copse. Beyond that, there was only open ground and, if they ventured out of the woods, he was sure he'd be able to shoot them down before they could reach the road.

He soon caught a glimpse of light coming through the trees up ahead. The tracks were still heading that way. If they hid in the woods, they could ambush him and get lucky, he supposed, but on open ground, it would be a different story; no surprises, no luck involved.

When he reached the edge of the trees and stared out over the moors, he was disappointed because all he could see was a vast open space. No runners out there. His confidence dipped. Had he misjudged his quarry? The trail they'd left had been so clear he wondered now whether that had been a deliberate ploy on their part. Maybe they'd led him here, then doubled back in an attempt to confuse him.

While he was puzzling it out, something moved in the bracken no more than twenty feet away. He thought it must be an animal and hurled a piece of wood but whatever was lurking there didn't up and run. Staring harder, he saw something lift when the wind gusted and, to gain a better view, shinned up a tree. From that vantage point two patches of colour stood out against the bracken and he permitted himself a smile of satisfaction.

Back on the ground again, he moved confidently out of the tree line, halted yards from where he was certain they were lying, a position near enough to put a bullet in them without the slightest risk to himself.

'Daddy's here!' he shouted. 'He can see you.'

He expected them to panic and run, was

surprised when nothing happened. A strange sense of foreboding came over him then, but he quickly shook it off because nothing could go wrong. He had them completely at his mercy with nowhere to run or hide.

Hurst decided to end it, raised his gun, took aim and sprayed the anoraks with bullets. As he advanced to make sure they were dead, it struck him as strange that neither the man nor the woman had moved or cried out. When he reached the spot, he soon realized why. There were no bodies there. He'd been shooting at two anoraks and, as he understood how he'd been deceived, a male voice came from behind.

'Drop the gun or I'll shoot you down where you stand!'

Hurst froze, cursing himself for his foolishness. He figured the guy must have picked up Frost's weapon. Why hadn't he thought of that possibility? Was it age creeping in? He decided he had nothing to lose and instead of dropping his gun as he'd been told, he lowered it to his side and turned slowly around.

He recognized the girl, but not the man pointing the weapon. Hurst could see the anger in his face, the slight tremble in his gun hand.

'Should have shot me in the back while you

had the chance,' Hurst said. 'Now you've only got a slight advantage and I'm good at this kind of thing.'

His words didn't seem to have much effect. The guy just looked at him as though he was the lowest creature on earth and Hurst was afraid he was fired up enough to pull the trigger before he could tip the scales further in his own favour.

'I told you to drop the gun. Do it now!'

Hurst smiled. He figured this guy wasn't going to be pliable and he'd have to take the chance on being better than him, which he was almost sure he would be.

'As if!'

He made his move, raised his arm fast, the way he had done a thousand times before, the way he'd been trained to by experts.

Before he could squeeze the trigger, something struck his shoulder with the force of a heavyweight's punch. The pain he felt there was matched a second later by another, which seared through his thigh muscle and burrowed into the bone like a drill. He dropped the gun, staggered like a newborn calf fighting for balance, then finally dropped down on one knee. Sure that at any minute a bullet would finish him, he scanned the ground with his eyes, searching frantically for his lost weapon.

'Don't bother. You're done.'

The voice was hard-edged, contemptuous. It left Hurst in no doubt that, if he tried anything, this time he would die. But death was preferable to prison. No way did he want to end up behind bars for the rest of his days. Better to die here than that. In desperation, he scanned the ground again and thought lady luck might give him one more chance when he spotted the gun. If he could get the gun and kill the guy, maybe he'd have enough strength to make it to the road and commandeer a car.

He reached out for the gun but before he made it a boot struck his jaw and sent him sprawling with a universe of stars coruscating behind his eyes. His survival instinct took over. Fighting his pain, he forced himself up onto his knees, shook his head in an attempt to banish those stars. When he managed to focus, he found himself looking down a gun barrel, the face behind it as cold and unforgiving as an ice field. He just had to ask.

'Why? Who are you?'

His nemesis drew a deep breath. 'I was a soldier . . . like my mates. The ones you killed.'

The words were spoken through gritted teeth. Hurst remembered a time when he'd been proud to call himself a soldier. It seemed so long ago, in another life.

'Finish it,' he said. 'I lived by the sword and that's how I want to die.'

He was sure this time he'd do it, that there was enough hate in that face, but he'd forgotten about the woman, who stepped forward and pleaded with him.

'No, Danny!'

The soldier didn't flinch.

'Why not? Scum like him don't deserve to be alive.'

Hurst decided to push him harder, before the woman convinced him.

'Would've killed that little bitch as well. Would've taken pleasure in it, like I did with your friends.' He forced a laugh. 'Would do it all again, too.'

The soldier's gun arm tensed. Hurst hoped he'd said enough to provoke him because the pain was becoming unbearable, his blood now weeping freely from his wounds onto the bracken.

'You heard him,' the soldier moaned. 'He's nothing.'

'Don't be like him,' the woman implored.

'Don't listen to her, man,' Hurst fired back, getting anxious now. 'I can tell you've done it before. What's one more to you?'

As he finished speaking, Hurst glimpsed a figure that looked like a ghost behind the

191

couple and wondered whether it was blood loss making him hallucinate. When the figure spoke, he knew it was no ghost but flesh and blood.

'Put the gun down, Danny!'

The man and woman turned in unison. Sounding relieved, the woman spoke up.

'That's DI Graham, Danny, please listen to him!'

'Let me take care of him, son,' the policeman said.

The soldier stared at the policeman, then at the gun in his own hand. Hurst was sure his anger was waning and with it his resolve. Cursing the woman and the policeman for interfering, he tried to provoke him again, spitting his words with as much contempt as he could muster.

'So much for loyalty to your mates, soldier boy. Can't even take revenge for them, can you?'

His words were wasted. Like a child suddenly losing interest in a toy, the soldier let the woman take the gun from him and just stared at the ground. She handed the weapon to the policeman, who, in turn, eyed Hurst so disdainfully he wondered whether he might pull the trigger himself.

'Save the taxpayers some money, pig,' Hurst groaned. 'You know you want to. I'll make a move and you can call it self-defence.'

The policeman raised his eyebrows. 'You must be a mind reader. I'm sure these people wouldn't object and there's nothing I'd like better after seeing your handiwork.' He scratched the back of his head with his free hand. 'But there couldn't be anything to come back on me later, no loose ends, no unanswered questions.'

Hurst thought he was having a sick joke, didn't think an officer of the law would take the risk of killing him. But this copper was still looking at him as though he would like to wipe him off the face of the earth.

'You serious, copper?'

'Deadly.'

Hurst decided to play along and hope. He had nothing to lose and there were no questions he wasn't prepared to answer.

'Go ahead and ask those questions.'

'I need to know why you killed Billy Hall and John Boyle.'

'Contract killings. Our boss is a man called Max. He hires us out. Don't know anything else.'

The policeman pointed towards Danny and Liz.

'How do they come into the equation?'

'Girl was a witness. The soldier . . . don't know a thing about him.'

'Last question. Where's your partner?'

'I killed him after the soldier stuck a knife in him. He's back there in the woods.'

The policeman smiled in a self-satisfied way. Hurst took that to mean it was the end of the questions, hoped he was going to keep his side of the bargain. But all the copper did was reach inside his jacket and withdraw his phone.

'Get all that recorded did you, Sandra?'

With a gleam of triumph in his eyes, he met Hurst's puzzled gaze.

'Good girl,' he said into the phone. 'I'll meet you at The Sailor Inn, soon as.'

It took him a moment but Hurst wasn't so far gone he didn't catch on. Letting go a string of expletives, he glared at the policeman.

'More honour among thieves . . . ' he muttered.

The policeman held the phone in the air like a trophy.

'It's all recorded just as I hoped. An ambulance and a helicopter are already on the way here so you might even live to die in prison.'

Hurst's hopes plummeted. There was no way out. He could already see grey walls, narrow cells with barred windows, years of mind-numbing routine, an infinitesimal chance of escape. Certain men might adapt but he knew he wasn't of that calibre. Yearning for a life outside would drive him insane. That policeman, curse him, could have given him the easy way out. Now, it would have to happen by his own hand. One day a screw would open his cell, find him lying there, blood streaming from his wrists, or hanging from the bars, head lolling, tongue protruding. It was a grim prognosis. Yet, even now, in that moment of terrible prescience, the nearest he came to regret for the life he'd led was wishing he'd quit while he was ahead.

A familiar sound interrupted his brooding and made him look up. A helicopter was approaching and it transported him back in time to those army missions in Iraq an age ago. As the cacophonous whirr of its rotor blades grew louder, he remembered how, in a tough spot, that sound had meant salvation, as though an angel were descending from the heavens to whisk them out of danger. Today it wasn't like that at all. Today the helicopter was a dark avenger, a harbinger of his destruction.

The bracken danced in the helicopter's downdraft. Armed men poured out of its belly and crouched low as they ran clear of the blades. While the others gathered in a circle, one of their number approached.

Hurst couldn't hear the conversation he held with the policeman but when they'd finished the newcomer gave a signal and two men came forward carrying a stretcher. Hurst submitted to an examination of his injuries before they lifted him onto the stretcher. As they carried him away, the policeman called out sarcastically.

'Aren't you the lucky one? You'll be in hospital before you know it. After that . . . prison.'

Hurst glared at him. 'Thanks for nothing!'

'My pleasure,' the policeman told him. 'Dying would be the easy way out for a man like you and there's a woman you widowed who'd think the same as me.'

*　*　*

The morning after his adventure on the moors Alex made his way bright and early to James Cook Hospital. The Hunt couple had been taken there more as a precaution than anything and he hadn't yet had the chance to question them. During the helicopter flight, the killer had started to bleed profusely, hadn't been in any condition to answer questions. Alex hoped to get down to business this morning and left a message at headquarters asking Sandra to meet him at

196

the hospital, thinking she might be of help when he questioned Liz Hunt.

As he walked towards the main building, it struck him how this whole business could so easily have had a more gruesome outcome. When he left the cottage he'd paused on top of the ridge, taken a last look back. That was when luck came into play because from his vantage point he'd seen a man and a woman run out of the copse, lay their coats on the bracken and dash back. He'd made a bee-line for the copse, arriving just in time to persuade Danny to hold fire.

Passing through the labyrinth of corridors, he felt satisfied with the way things had turned out. Delighted that his DI had thwarted two contract killers who were preparing to kill again, Smithers had been fulsome in his praise. But in his heart Alex knew the job was only half done because whoever had instigated the killings wasn't paying the price. All he had was the name Max. But who was paying Max? It would take more digging to really solve this case and he figured Danny Hall would be a good place to start because he was sure that young man knew something.

Danny was in a private ward. Alex showed the nurse on duty his warrant card, stepped through the door and found the patient lying with his hands behind his head and staring at the ceiling as though pondering a momentous problem. The scraping sound as Alex pulled up a chair caught his attention and the faraway look in his eyes soon disappeared when he realized who was visiting him.

'I owe you a big thank you, Inspector,' he said, sheepishly. 'I could easily have pulled the trigger after what they did to my friends and the terror they put us through. You saved me from myself.'

Alex smiled. 'My bet is you wouldn't have killed him, not like that, anyway. Can understand why you were tempted, though.'

'I hope you're right,' Danny said. 'I wouldn't like to be like them.'

Alex cleared his throat. There were other matters he needed to explore with this young man, delicate matters.

'It isn't finished, you know, not until I find who hired those men to have your pals killed . . . You must want that as well and I've a strong feeling you might be able to help.'

Pursing his lips, Danny turned his face away but Alex had seen enough to recognize the look of someone who has a secret he wants to tell but is afraid of the consequences. He'd seen it before, most usually on the face of a criminal tempted to confess his part in a crime but fighting it because it went against the grain.

'Whatever it is, get it off your chest, Danny. I'm sure you'll feel better if you do.'

Danny cast his eyes downward, clenched his fists, gave a woeful sigh.

'I promised Liz I'd tell the truth . . . but it isn't easy . . . it's not straightforward.'

'Not everything is black and white, son. I'm aware of that. But usually there's a right way to go.' Alex leaned in. 'What I need to know is who wanted your pals killed and why. You were out there on the moors when it all kicked off and I've a feeling that was a deliberate avoidance tactic on your part, though you probably didn't expect whatever they were involved in to lead to their murders.'

Danny's eyes flashed in his direction. He'd obviously hit the right nerve but for a moment he thought he was going to be stubborn. He was wrong, however, because it didn't take long for his story to come pouring out.

'Blackmail!' Danny spat the word out like a mouthful of bad wine that had soured his palate. 'My mates became blackmailers. I couldn't believe it.'

'And that's why they were assassinated?'

'Nearly sure it was.' Fire sparked in Danny's eyes. 'And I think I know who was behind it.'

Alex sighed. 'If you know who paid this guy Max, let's have it.'

Danny frowned, suddenly looked much older than his years. Alex could see he was struggling but didn't push it and finally his patience was rewarded as, with a resigned sigh, he began to unburden himself.

'The colonel. I think he arranged for them to be killed.'

Alex was so surprised he wondered whether he'd heard correctly.

'Surely you don't mean Lieutenant Colonel Martin?'

Danny nodded. 'The very same.'

Alex was flummoxed. On the two occasions they'd met, he'd found nothing to like about the colonel. He'd seemed cold and distant, hardly a charismatic leader. On hearing about the murders, he hadn't shown much feeling, hadn't seemed very keen to help, either. That reaction fitted a guilty man. But what possible motive could he have?

'Are you telling me your mates had something on him and because of it he had them assassinated? Is that what you're saying?'

Now that he'd taken that first step, Danny seemed much less hesitant, as though he'd bottled up his secret too long and was glad to be rid of it.

'It started with a photograph, Inspector. I

took it months ago and I wish I hadn't. It's hidden in the cottage.'

Alex reached into his jacket, slid out a brown envelope, handed it to him.

'I assume this is what you're referring to?'

Danny gave him a quizzical look then opened the envelope and pulled out the photograph. As he studied it, Alex explained how it had come into his possession.

'I searched the cottage. Since it was hidden, I thought it must be important. Seems I was right but for the life of me I can't see why.'

Seeing the photograph of his dead pals upset Danny and his face was melancholy as he placed it on the bed. When he'd composed himself, he spoke in a tone that was a mixture of nostalgia and regret.

'I took it the night young Robert Walker died. It was a week before my pals and I were due to leave the army and a gang of us arranged a night out in Middlesbrough — a last hurrah. Robert came with us.'

Danny paused, drew breath. Alex felt a surge of adrenaline. He already knew about the night out in Middlesbrough. Robert's trail had gone dead in the town, no CCTV images or anything helpful. As the night wore on and the drink flowed, the soldiers splintered off into smaller groups. At some point Robert slipped away, disappeared like a ghost without anybody noticing his absence. The night seemed to have just swallowed him up and spat him out again on that country road not so far from where Jamie had been killed. Was Danny about to enlighten him about the young soldier's fate? He hoped the way he was staring into space, as though his brain had gone absent without leave, didn't mean he was going to clam up.

'Come on, Danny, son, don't hold back on me now. Do you know something about Robert's disappearance? Is that it?'

His words got through. Danny emerged from the haze that had engulfed him and jabbed the photograph with his finger.

'Look in the background . . . there's a car. The figure leaning in the passenger window is Robert Walker. John Boyle put an arrow there pointing to him.'

Alex snatched the photograph up, studied the figure Danny had indicated. The face was fuzzy but whoever it was wore a tee-shirt with some words embossed on the front. Robert, he remembered, had been wearing a tee-shirt on that fateful night with Yorkshire Regiment printed on it. But he couldn't make out the words in the photograph and, frustrated, snapped his eyes back to Danny.

'It could be anybody, couldn't it?'

Danny sighed. 'You need a magnifying

glass. Billy used one. It's Robert all right, more's the pity.'

'That night Robert was wearing a regimental tee-shirt he'd bought from the NAAFI?'

'Exactly! That becomes clear under the glass, too. It's always a novelty for the newer recruits to wear them.'

Alex's hopes rose again. 'What about the car? Any ideas?'

'It's impossible to make out the driver but you can see it's a blue Mazda and the number plate is clear enough. The three of us knew the car and the number.' Danny drew in a deep breath, looked straight into Alex's eyes. 'It's the colonel's car, Inspector.'

That last piece of information shook Alex to his core. If, under closer examination, all this was true, it meant the colonel was probably the last person to see Robert Walker that night and hadn't revealed the fact, which was very suspicious to say the least. All those months of frustration and now, right out of the blue, this had landed on his plate when he'd had no expectations and was beginning to lose hope. Even better, if blackmail was involved, it could well be a motive linked to the other murders.

'Why didn't you come straight to us with this, Danny?'

Danny lowered his head, brought it up

again slowly. Shame coloured his cheeks a deep shade of red.

'It was three months later, when we were looking through old photos, that we spotted the car. That was when we realized it was Robert standing next to it. We figured the colonel had to know something about that night and, for some reason, hadn't told the police. My mates decided he must have something to hide. They were down on their luck in civvy street so made up their minds they would make the colonel pay for their silence.'

'And you wouldn't go along with that?'

'No way! I argued against it, wouldn't even let them have the photograph. It seemed to work because they appeared to have forgotten about it. Then, one night, about two weeks ago, the matter came up again and I couldn't persuade them to leave it alone this time.'

'But they didn't have the photograph, did they?'

Danny shook his head. 'They said it made no odds. It was enough that it existed. The colonel didn't have to see it, only believe they had it in their possession.'

Alex sighed. 'And still you didn't come to us!'

Danny met his gaze. A tear appeared in the corner of his eye, escaped onto his cheek, hovered there, not sure which direction to take. More tears came, ran down both cheeks leaving trails like scars. Alex watched him wipe them away and decided the patient needed a break.

'I'm going to pop outside for a ciggy,' he said, flashing what he hoped was a reassuring smile. 'You've done really well, Danny. We can continue this when I've had my fix.'

* * *

Alex didn't smoke, never had. That had just been an excuse to leave the ward because he hadn't liked watching a man who had braved the terrors of Afghanistan weeping and wanted to save the ex-soldier embarrassment.

The corridor was silent as he leaned against the wall mulling over what he'd just learned. He couldn't for the life of him imagine a reason why a high-ranking officer should have anything to do with the murder of one of his young soldiers, unless there was a homosexual affair going on and perhaps jealousy involved, but he didn't think that was a likely scenario. Anyway, that was getting ahead of himself because, even if it was the colonel's car in that alley, it would still be hard to prove the vital fact that it was the man himself in the driving seat that night.

The click of high heels coming along the

corridor encroached on his thoughts. He looked in their direction and saw Sandra Best striding towards him, wearing a blue coat and holding a bunch of flowers. In a corridor that lacked colour, she was like a bright vision. Straightening up, he stepped forward to meet her.

'What have I done to deserve those?' he said, pointing to the flowers. 'Don't tell me I've won policeman of the month again?'

Sandra pulled a face. 'Wake up and smell the coffee, boss. I bought these for Liz Hunt. She needs a bit of cheer in her life after what she's been through.'

'I never would have thought of that. Nice touch.'

'Don't worry, you'll be paying half.' Sandra smiled and nodded towards the ward door. 'You been in with Danny yet?'

'Yeah. Things got emotional. Tell you later. Just giving him a break.'

'Want me to come in?'

'Prefer it if you went to Liz and had a friendly little chat before we get down to the serious stuff. I'll join you when I've finished here.'

She made to go, then hesitated. 'They are going to be all right, aren't they? They seem like decent people and that phone call I recorded proved Danny wasn't involved.'

'Think they will. So far so good, anyway. Danny killed in self-defence. Liz was wrong to run from the safe house but her motive was innocent, so don't suppose much will happen about it.'

Sandra nodded. 'That's good, then.'

She reached inside her pocket, pulled out a large bar of Cadbury's chocolate, passed it to him. With a puzzled frown, he took it from her.

'You softening me up for something?'

'It's for you to give to Liz,' she said. 'Me the flowers, you the chocolate.'

He laughed. 'Beware of she who comes bearing gifts!'

'See you in a bit,' she said and turned away, muttering loud enough so he could hear. 'Policeman of the month indeed!'

After she disappeared, the corridor seemed colourless again, as though it mourned her absence. Or was that just him?

★   ★   ★

'Sorry about that,' Danny said as soon as Alex resumed his position at his bedside. 'I'm embarrassed.'

Alex looked him in the eye. 'Been there myself. Doesn't make you any less a man. We're none of us automatons, are we? After what you've been through you'd hardly be human if you weren't deeply affected.'

Those understanding words seemed to make a difference to Danny because he cheered up and held the Inspector's gaze.

'Thanks for that,' he said. 'It's hard not to get emotional when I think of how I've been to hell and back with Billy and John. They watched my back a thousand times and I wouldn't be alive now if it wasn't for them. We saw things, did things . . . ' His voice trailed off and he bit his bottom lip as though he wanted to inflict pain on himself to divert his thoughts. 'We have a pal who lost his legs. They said they wanted the blackmail money for him, too, that he would get his share. That made me feel bad. I wanted to come to the police but — '

Alex finished it for him. 'You ran away to the cottage instead.'

Danny dropped his eyes guiltily.

'They told me they'd done it and were waiting for the money so I thought I'd distance myself to get a clearer perspective, decide what to do. But I know now I was just running away from it all, avoiding a decision. Deep down I knew the right thing was to go to the police.' His eyes widened as though a sudden thought had struck him unexpectedly. 'My God, they wouldn't be dead now if I'd come to you straight away, would they?'

Alex shrugged. 'Once they started down that route there was no telling what could happen, how it would all end.'

Danny didn't look convinced. Alex felt sorry for him. He could understand how long-standing bonds of loyalty, tried and tested in extreme circumstances that not many could imagine, had undermined his law-abiding instincts. It seemed a shame that he would have to suffer for a decision that, while misguided, was based on a loyalty that was admirable in a way.

'My wife doesn't know yet,' he suddenly blurted out, looking crestfallen. 'Will you let me tell her myself before she hears it from someone else . . . before you . . . arrest me?'

'No problem with that. But first, is there anything else I need to know?'

Danny brought his hands together, interlocked his fingers and lowered his head like a penitent humbling himself before a confession to a priest. He remained silent for a long time while Alex waited, aware he was struggling with an inner turmoil. Finally, he decided Danny needed encouragement to rid himself of whatever was weighing on him so heavily.

'The truth will set you free, lad, but that means the whole truth. Believe me, if there's something, you'll feel better when it's out.'

At last, Danny raised his head. As though each word was costing him pain, he spoke in a low monotone.

'There's something I haven't told you about the colonel and . . . my wife.'

Now Alex really was puzzled. Was Danny about to announce that his wife was having an affair with his commanding officer? It would be an unlikely pairing, especially given the age difference, but he'd seen enough in his line of work and nothing would really surprise him. But it turned out the truth was equally, if not more surprising than that.

'The colonel is my wife's father,' Danny announced, his voice flat.

It was a bolt from the blue Alex could never have seen coming and, as he came to terms with it, he began to understand that Danny's problem must have been more complicated than had so far emerged. Danny had been a corporal at the lower end of the army hierarchy. A corporal marrying his colonel's daughter would be a scandal to some of those higher up who prided themselves on their rank and the social status that went with it. They would have considered it a blow to the status quo, a lowering of standards that had to be maintained at all costs. If he knew his man, the colonel would be devastated by the marriage.

'Tell me if I have this right,' Alex said. 'You didn't come to us because you were trying to be loyal to your mates . . . but also felt you had a certain loyalty to the colonel, your father-in-law, were reluctant to implicate him?'

Danny's eyes bulged in their sockets as he turned towards the detective and fired his words into the air like missiles.

'I've no loyalty to that man!'

Alex had disliked the colonel almost at first sight, didn't find it difficult to accept that Danny apparently felt the same way about him.

'My loyalty is to Liz,' Danny continued, softening his tone. 'She ran away from him when she was seventeen and I looked after her. The colonel never knew where she was or that she was with me. We worked very hard at being secretive, only married when I left the service. My mates knew I had a girlfriend but I never introduced her. They only met her recently and didn't know who she was because they'd only seen her very occasionally from a distance and she was away at boarding school in her teenage years.'

'So you wanted to protect your wife from the truth about her father. Is that it?'

Danny slumped back on the pillows, stared ruefully at the ceiling, as though he could see all his troubles parading there in visible form.

'I didn't want to be the one to go to the police. Have his name — her name — dragged through the mud. She'd suffered enough because of him. To have a murderer for a father . . . If that were true, just imagine. How could she tell her future children that their grandfather . . . ?'

Danny dried up, but he'd said enough for Alex to understand his dilemma; he'd been caught in a crossfire of loyalties; loyalty and his conscience clashing at a time when he was vulnerable himself. Standing back from it all, it was easy to see the right thing to do was inform the police, but Danny's involvement was personal and that had blurred the thin line that divided right and wrong.

'I made everything worse, didn't I?' Danny said, his voice plaintive. 'By not doing the right thing.'

What he'd said was true, but Alex could see there was much to be said in mitigation and found himself sympathizing, especially when it was clear he was punishing himself.

'When you left for the cottage, you couldn't have expected things to turn out so tragically, couldn't have foreseen those hit men going after your pals or your wife.'

'But I was wrong,' Danny said, 'that's all that counts. It makes me an accessory. They'll send me to prison for that, won't they?'

Somewhere in the recesses of Alex's mind an idea had already been lurking, which he hadn't allowed to come too far forward, but now it began to insist and he couldn't dismiss it. He tried to tell himself it was a foolishness, a case of sentiment overcoming reason, but it wouldn't let go. He knew if he pursued it, he'd need to be careful, cover all the angles, not to mention his own back.

'Apart from yourself, nobody else knew what your mates were planning. Is that right, Danny? It's important I know.'

'No! They weren't even going to tell our pal Jackie, the one who lost his legs.'

Alex slid his hand over the sheet towards the photograph. His fingers hovered for a moment before he made his decision, then he swept it up and put it inside his pocket, praying he was doing the right thing.

'Listen carefully,' he said, transferring his gaze to Danny, 'and we might just be able to get you out of this mess.'

'How . . . ?' Danny interrupted, his mouth dropping open.

'This is the new sequence of events,' Alex continued, thoughtfully, looking for flaws even as he explained. 'I found the photograph in John Boyle's flat, showed it to you today. Looking at it closely, you recognized the car and number plate. Together we used a magnifying glass and it became clear the figure near the car was none other than Robert Walker.' Alex paused. 'Get all that clear in your head and remember you gave the photo to your pal without knowing any of this at the time.'

Danny looked incredulous as it dawned on him that Alex was trying to help him.

'Why are you doing this?' he stuttered.

'Let's just say you never intended any harm, just misjudged the situation and I admire your loyalty.' Alex swallowed hard. 'That and the fact I had a son who would be about your age if he hadn't been killed. I hope someone would have given him a second chance if he needed one.'

Danny hung his head. 'You're risking a lot and I'm not sure I deserve it but I won't forget this . . . ever.'

'Just stick to that story, no matter what.'

Alex rose from the chair. There was more to his plan but he didn't think Danny would be enthusiastic about the rest of it.

'You do know the photo is only circum-stantial evidence, don't you?' he said. 'It proves nothing except that the colonel didn't come forward, though that in itself is damning. My bet is he'll claim he wasn't driving the car that night, something like that.

One way or another, he'll wriggle. Proving he was linked to those hit men would help but that won't be easy.'

Danny's eyes flashed at Alex on full beam. 'Could I have assumed too much thinking he set my mates up because they were blackmailing him? Could someone else have had a reason for killing them? Maybe he didn't murder Robert Walker.'

Alex shook his head. 'That's the line his barrister would probably take. I'm afraid we need more. There's a way to get the truth, given what you've told me, but I don't think you'd like it one bit.'

'Try me,' Danny said.

Alex outlined his plan, Danny looking increasingly concerned as he realized what it involved. The detective expected him to be wary, didn't blame him after what he and his wife had been through already. It was asking a lot of him and Liz but Alex didn't push it, simply gave him the bones to chew on, stressed that any danger would be minimized to an infinitesimal degree by police back-up. Danny's ambivalence was evident by his long silence.

'Look,' Alex said. 'When you speak to Liz, put it to her, see what she thinks, decide between you. I can understand if you decide to reject it and don't worry, we'll still stick to the sequence of events I outlined and say you had no involvement whatsoever.'

Danny sighed. 'That's fair enough. I've had enough of keeping things from my wife so I'll discuss it with her, see what she wants to do.'

'We'll see, then,' Alex said. He stood up and looked down at Danny. 'I wouldn't have suggested it if I thought there'd be great danger involved. The risk would be minimal.'

'Either way,' Danny said, 'I owe you more than I can ever repay.'

★　★　★

As he moved towards the door, Alex thought he saw the handle twitching. Icy fingers ran up and down his spine. Had someone been listening outside the door while he talked to Danny, heard him concoct the story? The nurses had been instructed to keep clear while police were visiting but one of them could have been listening. Cursing himself for his carelessness, he flung the door open and stepped out into the corridor.

He came to an abrupt halt when he saw Sandra Best. He knew instantly from her body language, the indecisive stance, the guilty look of a schoolgirl caught in a misdemeanour, that she'd heard something she was aware she wasn't meant to hear. Without a word, he took her by the arm, led her to a sofa next to the wall, told her to sit down, then lowered himself into the seat next to her while he tried furiously to think what he would tell her. The uncomfortable silence between them stretched out because she didn't seem to know what to say, either. Anyone who passed by would have thought them a long-married couple who didn't feel the need for idle talk. Still reproaching himself for his carelessness, Alex was the first to speak, his voice more clipped than he intended

'How much did you hear?'

'Enough.'

Colouring up, Alex forced himself to look at her, tried to read her expression but couldn't because it was deadpan. Figuring whatever needed to be said now should come from her, he waited quietly for her reaction.

'I didn't mean . . . ' she began. 'Liz was asleep. I left the flowers with a nurse, came back here, opened the door.' She hesitated, drew in a breath. 'It wasn't deliberate. I just got caught up in the moment, mesmerized by what you were saying.'

Annoyed with himself for placing her in such an awkward position, Alex muttered, 'I should have been more careful. Now I've compromised you.'

To his surprise, when she looked at him he

saw concern rather than condemnation.

'I didn't get it all, just the gist of it,' she stated. 'But enough to know you're taking a risk . . . a career-threatening risk that could send you to prison.'

He didn't need her to tell him that and, anyway, he'd made up his mind that this was one time when he needed to bend the rules and wasn't for turning.

'Danny Hunt will go to prison if I don't interfere,' he said. 'Maybe the court would consider the mitigating circumstances but wouldn't understand fully the emotions involved because they haven't seen them first hand. That lad was pulled in all directions. He didn't set out to do harm. He was thinking of other people and I think he deserves a break rather than a ruined life.'

'It's not your job — '

Alex thrust out his jaw. 'This is a one off, Sandra. They're a young couple just starting out in life.'

'Thought you always went by the book,' she riposted. 'As I recall that's what you taught me.'

'That was so you wouldn't make mistakes early in your career.'

She gave him a scathing look. 'And now, in your own mid-career, it's all right for you to risk everything?'

'I'll get through, cover all the angles,' he told her, evading her eyes. 'That is unless you feel duty-bound to report it. After all, I have compromised you and I wouldn't blame you for one moment.'

The ferocity behind the punch to his shoulder surprised him and so did the way she catapulted to her feet and looked down at him with what he thought was disdain. He'd seen her angry before but not like this and he couldn't understand why until she made it plain for him.

'How could you say that,' she scolded, 'when you know very well I'll do no such thing? I just hope for your sake and theirs you can pull it off.' She pulled her coat around her as though erecting a barrier between them. 'Now, are we going to interview Liz Hunt or are you afraid I'll snitch?'

Taken aback, he could only mutter, 'No need for that now, not until her husband talks to her.'

'In that case if you don't mind I'll be off back . . . on my own . . . boss.'

He nodded meekly, started to say something but she'd already turned her back on him. Surprised his suggestion had angered her to such an extent, he scratched his head in puzzlement and watched her flounce down the corridor.

* ⋆ ⋆

In her private ward Liz Hunt leaned back on her pillow and watched her husband come through the door. As he sat down beside the bed and took her hand, she noticed he looked tired and yet there was something brighter about him, as though he'd had an infusion of hope and today the world looked a better place than when they'd parted last night. After she'd reassured him she was doing fine, she fell silent, waiting for him to explain exactly what had been going on in his life that he hadn't been able to share with her.

Fiddling nervously with the cord of his dressing gown, he started by telling her he was ashamed of going off and leaving her in danger.

'Well, I'm sure you had your reasons,' she said, her tone conciliatory, 'and I'd like to hear them, and everything else that I don't know about.'

Danny stopped fiddling with the cord, stared at the wall behind her bed as though searching for an autocue that could help him find his words.

'First off,' he said, eventually, 'I'm really proud of you. I asked you to tell nobody where I was and you stuck to that. Believe me, I wouldn't have asked you to if I'd foreseen . . . ' He looked straight at her. 'You were more loyal than I deserved.'

'You're my husband, Danny, that's why I kept quiet.' She sighed. 'I confess I wondered sometimes whether I was doing the right thing. What really hurt me was you gave me no reasons. We'd always been a team, no secrets between us.'

Danny flinched, tightened his grip on her hand, a gesture she sensed was meant to reinforce the bridge between them that, though it still stood firm, had taken a battering.

'If you remember, before I left that day I told you my reason for taking time out involved you, Liz.'

She nodded. 'I couldn't understand what that could possibly mean. Even now I can't. At the time, I just thought whatever was getting to you automatically brought me into it.'

'There was no reason for you to understand. I wanted to keep it from you because I didn't want to hurt you.'

'Well, you'll have to tell me now, Danny.'

Her husband drew in a deep breath and began his tale. Liz did her best to keep her face impassive, though, as soon as Danny spoke about the suspicions he and the inspector harbored against her father, her mask slipped and she couldn't hide her incredulity. As her brain absorbed the truth and she came to understand the reasons behind her husband's aberrant behaviour, how loyalty to his friends and desire to protect her had kept him from going to the police, her heart went out to him. Surely he'd been through enough without all that fresh turmoil?

'You'll go to prison, Danny,' she sobbed.

He shook his head, told her how the inspector was prepared to risk his career to give him a second chance. She could hardly believe it.

'Not many would do that,' she said. 'Maybe your luck's changed, Danny.'

He opened his mouth to say something but held back, bit his lip nervously. His hesitation worried her.

'There's something else I have to tell you,' he said, eventually.

'You mean there's a catch?' He'd sounded so reluctant she felt her new-found hope already starting to dissipate. 'I might have known. Happy endings only happen in films.'

'You're wrong, Liz,' he said. 'The inspector made it crystal clear he wasn't imposing any conditions; he just wanted your help with something if you were agreeable. I was reluctant but told him I'd discuss it with you and we'd decide together. You don't have to do it and in my opinion you shouldn't.'

Liz made an effort to shrug off an instant stab of scepticism. 'I think you'd better tell me what he wants and then we'll see how the land lies.'

Danny explained and, as he spoke, Liz had a strange feeling that, however reluctant she might be to embrace it, her destiny was seeking her out and she would have to comply because she was the only one who could do it. It helped that she felt only resentment towards a man who had never loved her the way a father should a daughter.

'I don't want you to do it,' Danny said, 'and you don't have to.'

Her reply was clear and firm. 'If I don't the truth may never come out and that makes it a moral obligation, so I'm going to do it, Danny.'

Danny looked doubtful. 'Whatever I say won't make any difference, will it?'

'Afraid not,' she said, 'and besides we really do owe Inspector Graham a big favour.'

⋆   ⋆   ⋆

Liz hesitated at the door of the cottage, childhood memories revolving in her head, most of them ugly. It was one of the last places she'd have visited without compelling reason. Her father had bought it when he'd been promoted to major and it had been the family home. Now, as she stood on the threshold in fading light, her emotions vacillated between nostalgia — when she recalled her mother's presence here — and regret and old anger at the callous way her father had treated both of them. She found it hard to raise her hand and lift the door knocker, knowing that act would open a portal to a part of her past she'd confined to a prison in her memory where her resentment was best left under lock and key. As she tried to overcome her inertia, Danny flashed into her mind and, at that moment, more than ever before she understood her husband's struggle to come to terms with those terrible memories of Afghanistan. Paradoxically, it was nurturing Danny over the years that had made her strong, given her the courage to face this moment.

Gathering her courage, she raised her hand and knocked; the sound of metal on wood echoed inside the cottage like a preliminary salvo before the main battle.

As though the lid of a tomb was suddenly shifting after lying undisturbed for centuries, the door creaked slowly open and a face she had buried long ago appeared. Other than a raised eyebrow, not a flicker of emotion registered on her father's stern features and not a word emerged from his lips. His eyes inspected her head to toe as though she were a soldier on the parade ground rather than a daughter he hadn't seen or heard from in five years. She could feel that old coldness emanating from him like winter's first bite and she knew he hadn't changed from the man she'd known. In a way, that was a relief; it would make her mission here much easier.

'Aren't you going to ask me in?' she said, taking the initiative, surprised there was strength in her voice she didn't really feel, that her trepidation at having to face her tyrant of a father once again, though not far below the surface, was well disguised.

He still didn't speak, nor did his expression change as he pushed the door wide open, turned his back and retreated inside.

Liz took a deep breath and followed him through to the kitchen where he leaned against the sink, arms folded, watching her like a teacher might an errant pupil who has come to him to confess a wrongdoing. She positioned herself on the other side of the rectangular table, which, given their anti-pathy, might as well have been an ocean of ice. Cold eyes willed Liz to speak first, to beg forgiveness and it couldn't have been more plain that he didn't regard her as a returning prodigal worthy of the fatted calf, that his inflexibility encompassed those years apart. But she wasn't a child any more. Instead of crumbling, she refused to be intimidated and returned his stare, determined she was going to win the battle of wills. This time she won and he succumbed to her, but his resentment was clear in the way he fired questions at her with sneering self-righteousness.

'Money? Pregnant and deserted? Drug addict? All three, perhaps?'

His terseness added to the sting in the words. Liz's anger suffused even though she had expected no less from this sanctimonious martinet whom she'd had the misfortune to have as a father. She calmed herself with the knowledge that it didn't matter a jot given the magnitude of the sins she was here to expose. Even so, she couldn't maintain her former coolness and came straight to it.

'How can you talk like that when you're nothing but a murdering bastard?'

As he glowered at his daughter, under the glare of the kitchen lights the colonel's cheeks were as flushed as two robins' breasts. Like a seminal moment in the theatre that induces a hush in the audience, a silence heavy with implication settled on the room.

Liz kept watching her father. The nerve in his temple was twitching as though a worm was wriggling under his taut skin. His cheeks were struggling to confine the blood pooling there. She was sure her direct approach had thrown him and he was ready to explode. Yet, she could see something else there too, something she couldn't remember seeing before, a flash of fear in his cold eyes, which was constricting him. He was studying her as though he wanted to strike her and was struggling to restrain the impulse. Undaunted, she continued her attack, reaching inside her jacket for the photograph the inspector had given her and slapping it down on the table like a gauntlet.

'Take a good look,' she said, 'and then deny that you're a murderer.'

He was perfectly still for a moment, each muscle tense, like an animal preparing itself to spring, then he reached out, snatched up the photograph. Liz watched his reaction as he studied it, the throb rising and falling in his throat, the red tide receding from his face leaving a bleached-white pallor.

'What can you mean?' he said, in a scoffing tone, but a hoarseness in his voice betraying his discomfiture. 'I recognize two of my former men in that photograph and that's it.' He paused, eyes betraying his slyness. 'How did you get it?'

Liz laughed mirthlessly. 'That's your car in the background and Robert Walker is talking to you. You remember him, don't you? You should! He was one of your young soldiers murdered the night that photograph was taken. You didn't come forward and that begs a question, doesn't it?'

'Don't be ridiculous,' the colonel came back at her, straightening his shoulders. 'The picture isn't clear. It could be any car, anyone driving and anyone standing there next to it. I repeat, how did you get it? Who put you up to this outrage?'

Liz ignored his questions. 'The number plate is clear enough. It's your car, all right, and using a magnifying glass, it's easy to see it is Robert Walker.'

Her father averted his eyes but not quickly enough to hide the fluttering of fear she'd noted before. When he looked at her again it had gone, but had been replaced by an animal cunning, which frightened Liz. When he spoke, his voice was a low rumble, threatening thunder to come.

'Who gave you the photograph? Who put this madness into your head?'

'Doesn't matter who!' she fired back, suppressing her fear. 'It won't alter anything and, if I tell you, they'll likely end up murdered . . . just like the men in the photograph who tried to blackmail you.'

This time, like an invading parasite, fear

took up residence in his eyes. Liz knew then, if she'd ever doubted it, he was guilty and that she'd shocked him to his core. He opened his mouth but nothing came out. Never before had she seen him lost for words, nor that old man's droop to his shoulders. She was sure it was beginning to dawn on him that no dissembling on his part would work, that she had him in the palm of her hand.

'If you know so much,' he muttered, trying to rally, 'why haven't you gone to the police? Surely not because of any filial loyalty to your dear papa.'

Liz looked at him steadily. This was it, the moment to gamble, to make him admit his sins.

'My husband came to me with this photograph. He wouldn't join in the plan to blackmail you; he only told me about it after I accidentally witnessed the death of one of his pals and your hired men started to hunt me. He wouldn't go to the law because you were my father and he thought it would hurt me, and any kids we have in the future would be affected. Unlike you, he has a touch of nobility about him.'

A glimmer of hope entered her father's eyes. She knew it was because she'd dangled a way out of his predicament in front of him.

'Husband? What husband?'

'I married a soldier, the same lad you tried to prevent me seeing. For some reason, he thought he should protect me from knowing about my murderous father.'

She knew how pragmatic his mind was, how every decision was led by self-interest. She could see his brain ticking over, trying to work out a way for him to wriggle off the hook. Finally, he came up with the answer she was half expecting.

'You and your husband want money just like those other two. That's the reason for all this, isn't it?'

She despised him even more for his transparency. It was time to be blunt, draw him out further.

'You know your daughter so well, don't you? Of course that's what I want, but something else, too. I want to know why you killed a young man like Robert Walker and then hired assassins to kill men who served you. I want to know what kind of man can do that.'

His eyes slid away, moved around the room. She noticed, now that he'd seen a possible way out, that his former composure seemed to be returning. In the silence, she waited anxiously for his answer. The seconds felt like minutes until, somewhere outside the cottage, an owl gave a derisory hoot and, as though prompting him, her father fixed his eyes on his daughter, kept them there wide and unblinking. It was designed to penetrate her defences, winkle out any subterfuge. Once, she would have withered under its laser-like intensity, but not any more.

'If I tell you, how can I be sure you won't go to the police?'

'Just think about it,' she said, feigning impatience. 'It would be all over the press and I've already told you I wouldn't want my children to discover their grandfather was a monster, a psychopath in the guise of an officer and gentleman. Bad enough my husband and I would have to carry that burden . . . correction: I already do carry it.'

For a moment, she thought she'd gone too far, ignited his temper enough for him to want to murder her too. But, as ever, his self-interest was paramount and guided his mood and decision.

'I'll tell you why I had to do it,' he said, 'and then we'll discuss money. You won't like what you hear but you might be consoled by the fact I was protecting your interests as well as my own.'

★   ★   ★

231

The blacked-out van was hidden amongst trees, couldn't be seen by the few cars that used the country road. In the back of the van, three men hunched together, heavy overcoats and microphones over their ears, a close verisimilitude of three bears in a huddle. They were staring at the tapes spinning in front of them as though they were entranced. But it wasn't the tapes so much as the words being recorded that commanded their full attention, words that were leading them to believe that their current discomfort wasn't going to be in vain.

Alex Graham was more edgy than both the young DC and the technician in charge of the machinery because he had instigated this operation. Liz Hunt had agreed to it without much hesitation and, so far, she was following the script they'd rehearsed, give or take one or two flourishes of her own, which worried Alex in case they provoked her father to the violence of which he believed him to be so eminently capable. After preliminary verbal fencing between father and daughter, the colonel had provided enough evidence to arrest him. The conversation had swung to motive now, the icing on the cake, as far as Alex was concerned.

'Got enough, haven't we, sir?' the young DC whispered in his ear, politely enough.

Alex wasn't sure what inspired the comment: fatigue, boredom or maybe just enthusiasm to get on with the arrest. Though he was strongly tempted to end it there himself, to curtail Liz Hunt's ordeal and make absolutely sure she came out of this unscathed, he shook his head.

'The more we have on him the better, so let's run with it. He knows her husband is aware of where she is and what she's doing so he won't dare try anything as long as she stays within the parameters we suggested.'

Alex wasn't as confident as he'd sounded. There was always an element of risk involved in these enterprises, often impossible to predict. This was a father and daughter confrontation but sometimes ego and self-interest superseded even ties of blood. That was why he was very much on edge, alert to the need to call in the troops hidden a little way up the road as soon as there was any sign that the colonel was ready to turn to violence. He didn't like riding so close to the wind, only hoped he'd be astute enough to make the call at the right moment if events inside the cottage took a nasty turn. Even though Liz and Danny had been made well aware of the risk, he'd never forgive himself if anything happened to her and neither would her husband.

Back in the cottage, Liz was confused. Was her father playing games? He'd claimed he'd been partly protecting her interests. That had to be a lie, an obvious ploy to ingratiate himself with her . . . as if there could be any chance of that happening. Little did he know he'd already condemned himself, that the hounds were close by and he was running unwittingly towards them with every word he uttered. When she spoke to him again, it was with the hope she could entice him to reveal the full extent of his evil machinations to those listening.

'Enlighten me, then, so that I know exactly what motive turned my father into a killer without a conscience.'

He declined his head, looked at her from under the hoods of his eyes.

'You had no idea you had a rival for my affections, did you, dear daughter?'

Liz wondered at the nerve of the man, prevaricating when he should have been weighed down with guilt. A rival for his affections? That was rich coming from him. He hadn't shown her or her mother affection, only his controlling nature that always put his needs first. Power had always been his first and last love, outward appearances more important than integrity.

'Get to the point!' she snapped, remembering how awful he'd made family life.

'Very well, then.' He pointed to the photograph on the table, smirked in a self-satisfied way that made her skin crawl.

'Tell me, Elizabeth, did you see anything familiar about Robert Walker, anything of yourself, perhaps?'

The question was so unexpected, so off base, it piqued her curiosity, but she was sure it was just a game he was playing, that he was about to concoct an elaborate lie to reassert his lost authority.

She shrugged, affected indifference.

'There's no reason I should.'

'Oh, but there is, Elizabeth, and that's where it all starts. You see I had to kill him to protect my position, my future and . . . my . . . our family name.' He glanced at her slyly as though something else had occurred to him that might help his cause. 'Besides, in spite of your falling spectacularly below all my expectations, you will — because of my actions — inherit all my wealth.'

His unctuous manner, so far from his true character, disgusted Liz. But she was mystified, too. Her father had spoken of a connection between her and Robert Walker and of her inheriting his money. Where was all that going? She was sure it would turn out to be a fabrication, an attempt to justify the unjustifiable. Yet, in spite of herself, she was intrigued.

'I'm not interested in your money,' she sneered, 'and you wouldn't do anything for me anyway. You killed that poor boy for reasons of your own, so let's hear the ugly truth without you embellishing it.'

Her words hit home. His lower lip protruded like a sulky child's and he clenched his fists together, familiar signs she remembered as preliminary to one of his tantrums. He was struggling to contain his real nature, staring at her as though he wanted to kill her but holding himself in check. She figured the reason for his self-restraint was that she'd told him, if he confessed to the truth, she wouldn't go to the police and his self-preservation instinct was well honed.

'I had an affair when you were little,' he said, in a clipped but matter-of-fact tone, that was, again, much more like his true self. 'Your mother never knew about it, nor about the child that resulted.' He gritted his teeth. 'That child was . . . adopted.'

He'd taken her by surprise, not with the affair, because she might have expected that, knowing him, but with news of the child she'd had no idea existed. After the initial shock, she thought back to everything he'd said and it led her to a dark place she didn't want to go. Voice strained, hoping that it was purely her imagination at work, she pre-empted her father.

'You're not going to tell me that Robert Walker . . . was your son . . . and you killed your own son . . . my brother. Tell me I've got that wrong.'

'Not brother, half-brother,' the colonel conceded. His tone carried no shame and implied the distinction made all the difference.

Her stomach churned. Bad enough he was a killer; now he was confessing to murdering his own flesh and blood.

'How could you? Not even an animal — '

Meeting her gaze, he cut her short. 'Hear me out and I'm sure you'll understand why.'

She knew she never would understand but, half dazed, she listened as he told her the child he had never met found out he was his father, joined the regiment and came to him demanding he recognize him as his son. He'd tried to tell him it would cause a scandal, ruin his career, but to no avail. On that fateful night, he'd picked him up in Middlesbrough, driven him into the country to discuss the matter, hoped to dissuade him with the promise of a large sum of money if he'd forget all about their relationship. The lad had become incensed and had thrown a tantrum, blaming him for the orphanages and foster homes he'd had to endure all his young life, all his other problems, too.

'He obviously had no backbone, was probably psychologically unbalanced,' the colonel said. 'He struck me so I picked up a stone and hit him in self-defence . . . didn't mean to kill him.'

Liz's face contorted as though a repugnant odour had assailed her nostrils. It was enough of a sin to have killed his own flesh and blood without lying about it, because she remembered the inspector mentioning the body had been struck more than was necessary to kill and probably with a baseball bat, which meant it was either premeditated murder or committed in a state of uncontrolled fury. The papers had reported as much.

'He was hit more than once, you lying bastard!'

The strength of her fury seemed to surprise him and his eyelids fluttered like a fledgling's wings.

'I panicked, Elizabeth! I had to do it!'

The way he used her name, the implied intimacy, grated. She didn't want anything to do with him, this beast of a man whose pathetic attempts to portray himself in a better light insulted her intelligence. From deep in her memory, all his cruelties to her mother came floating up to the surface. It wasn't hard for her to believe that he'd driven his son out into the country that night with murder already in his heart. He must have read her feelings because his tone changed again, became harder.

'I'm still your father and there'll be a momentous scandal. As you correctly pointed out, you and your children will suffer. The scandal will echo down the generations. But if you walk away now who will ever know? Life will go on as before. You have to see that, daughter.'

She held back from telling him she'd already decided to put justice before self-interest and was prepared for the sacrifice demanded of her and her future children. She'd do her best to protect them, of course, but she'd make them strong too, strong enough to cope with the knowledge a man like him was their progenitor. Evil men like her father couldn't be allowed to flourish under any circumstances, no matter how abhorrent the consequences. Now there was only one more question left to ask before she could walk away from him.

'How did you find those killers?'

He wafted a hand in the air. 'I knew a man in London who deals in matters of that nature. Goes by the name of Max Sinclair. No need to worry about that. He's discreet and the men he uses are professional assassins who'll cover their tracks.'

That was it, all the sordid details out in the open, all the participants named and shamed. It was time to leave. She wanted to tell him how much she loathed him, how he'd condemned himself out of his own mouth and would be punished by the law. But sadness for her mother, her wasted years with this tyrant that had probably contributed to her early death and her own regret that she had never known a loving father, came rushing out of the past in a vortex of emotion and it was all she could do to hold back her tears.

As she tried to get a grip, say what she'd been told to say and take her leave, a cry like an animal in pain came from beyond the door to the living room. Her father's head jerked upright and he stared at the door as though at any moment he expected it to be thrown open and something horrible to emerge from the bowels of the house.

★ ★ ★

Inside the van, in spite of the cold, sweat trickled down Alex's spine. The tapes were spinning away, recording the colonel's words which would later be used against him. Alex wondered, rather fancifully, if there was a heaven where celestial beings were tasked with recording each man's sins in preparation for a day he'd be called to account. No man was without sin, that was for sure, but he figured, from all they'd heard so far, the colonel would be near the top of the pile.

He wished he had the power to fast-forward time, get this business finished with because it seemed to be dragging. Liz Hunt was doing a good job but he could tell by the antagonism in her voice she was finding it difficult to keep her emotions in check, be entirely pragmatic in her approach. Who could blame her in the circumstances? His nervousness arose from concerns for her safety, though, from the way the colonel was opening up, he couldn't have any suspicions about his daughter's real purpose.

Liz elicited information about the hit men and Alex figured that was the business concluded, time for her to get out of there. The whole sad tale had been laid bare and the colonel was going to be put away for the rest of his life. Removing his headphones, he gave a sigh of relief. Soon Liz would leave the cottage and he'd be in there arresting the colonel, an act that was going to give him great satisfaction.

He tapped the young DC on the shoulder, waited until he'd removed his headphones before he spoke.

'Just about time for us to move in.'

The DC lumbered to his feet. He was as tall as Alex and they stood with their shoulders forward, heads bent to avoid touching the roof of the van.

'What about the armed response guys, sir?'

Alex shook his head. 'Leave them on standby. He's not suspicious or he wouldn't have confessed. She'll be out of there in a minute so we'll just stroll down there now, wait until she comes out then arrest him.'

Looking slightly disconcerted, the DC said, 'Just the two of us, sir?'

Alex shot him a quizzical look.

'Don't see anyone else around. My brain and your muscle should do it. No need to go in mob-handed.'

Alex stepped out of the van followed by the younger detective. After being cooped up in the van, like athletes at the end of a race both breathed in a lungful of air and stretched arms and legs that had become cramped. Then Alex led the way down the lane at a brisk pace.

'Hard to believe, isn't it, sir?' the younger man said when they'd gone a few yards.

'What is?'

'That somebody like that can rise to colonel, exercise all that power, send men into action . . . to their deaths.'

'Way of the world, son, a story as old as time. Power corrupts those who desire it for the wrong reasons and want to hold on to it at all costs — like our man there. He hesitated, then added, 'Policemen aren't immune, you know. We have our psychopaths hiding inside uniforms.'

'Think I've met one or two,' the DC said lugubriously.

They were only yards from the cottage which, to Alex, looked like an idyllic haven, the house lights twinkling in the dark, illuminating a well-kept garden. He supposed it could have passed for one of those cottages chosen for a calendar, the type that makes you envy the owners the peace and tranquility you imagine they must have found there. In this case, that definitely wasn't true and it just went to show appearances weren't everything, that it took more than bricks and mortar to make a happy home. Behind those walls, a daughter was facing a father and having to come to terms with unpalatable truths about him that no daughter should ever have to hear. Alex felt desperately sorry for her.

★ ★ ★

Liz's eyes darted between her father's frozen features and the door to the living room behind which that pitiful, ghostly sound had issued forth a moment ago. It was deadly quiet in the kitchen now except for the ticking of the clock on the wall. Liz remembered that clock from her childhood, how she'd imagined it as the heartbeat of the cottage. Now it conjured old ghosts, moments with her mother lost in time. Studying her father's face, she wondered what ghosts were wandering through his mind, how he managed to live with them. For sure, in the days and years ahead they would return to him in the confines of his prison cell, have their revenge.

Finally, the tautness left his facial muscles and he seemed to relax, though she thought she could detect a wariness that hadn't been there before and which had some connection to whatever they'd heard in the living room.

'Must have been a draught,' he said, more to himself than to her. 'It's an old cottage.'

The words were barely out of his mouth when the living room door flew open and, like a harridan released from hell itself, a woman with wild, grey hair and an insane look in her eye exploded into the kitchen. She was holding a shotgun like someone born to use it and she pointed it straight at the colonel, who, in a reflex response, held up his hands like a shield. The woman didn't seem to even notice Liz, so intently was she focused on her father.

'Bastard!'

As she pronounced the expletive, spittle flew from her mouth, landed on the table. Her hands started to shake so that the shotgun wavered like a divining rod.

'I heard everything! Do you hear me? Everything!'

Liz was rooted to the spot. She was sure that a wrong word or move from her might tip this woman, whoever she was, right over the edge because she seemed more like a wild animal than a human being; the cause of the hatred consuming her was an inexorable force.

Her father turned ashen. He was still cowering behind his hands, his mouth opening and shutting as he struggled to speak without success.

Finally, he managed to stammer, 'Please, Janet, don't. I did it for us . . . you and me. I'm . . . sorry.'

'Sorry!'

The woman threw back her head, laughed hysterically. For the first time, she looked at Liz, who noticed her eyes were glassy, like a drug addict's who inhabits a world of her own where no one else can enter.

'He says he's sorry!' she said, leveling the shotgun at the colonel. 'Sorry! Sorry! Sorry!'

The colonel recoiled, half turned away, pushing back against the sink. The woman's smile was as mirthless as a skull as she stepped around the table and prodded his chest with the barrel like a child tormenting an animal for the pure satisfaction derived from the act. He sank to his knees, clasped his hands together, a penitent at the feet of his confessor

'Please!' he sobbed.

'Don't!' Liz yelled, at last finding her voice. 'Whatever he's done to you, it's not worth ruining your life for him.'

Once again, those glassy eyes swung towards Liz, seemed to look right through her to a horizon far beyond the confines of the kitchen. When she spoke her voice changed, became soft and wistful.

'My baby came back to me first,' she cooed. 'It was the best day of my life. Robert wanted to introduce himself to his father and I thought he'd been killed before he had a chance.' Her voice changed again and she spat fury. 'I thought I was saving that bastard unnecessary grief keeping it from him but now I know he murdered his own flesh and blood!'

Wringing his hands together, her father

pleaded. 'I had to, Janet . . . for us. Don't you see it would have ruined us?'

She turned back to the colonel with a sneer of utter contempt. He broke down, started to sob as though he'd sensed there was no way back for him, nothing he could say that would appease this woman he'd wronged.

'I thought it was God's punishment for allowing you to let my baby go all those years ago, for marrying you even after that. But now I know it was you, not God. You're a cold, heartless beast and I've been a naïve, selfish woman. How I've paid for that.' She sighed, nodded in Liz's direction. 'No wonder your daughter rejected you!'

Liz took a deep breath. Powerful emotion, not least her bad conscience, was motivating the woman and it wouldn't be easy to dissuade her from using the weapon. But she knew she had to try.

'Believe me, he's going to pay,' she pleaded. 'He'll spend the rest of his life in prison thinking on his evil actions. I'm wired up and the police have recorded his confession. As soon as I step out the door they'll be in here to arrest him so please let them take care of it.'

The woman didn't seem to hear a word she'd said; either that or it didn't matter to her anyway. She seemed to have gone beyond reason and now raised the weapon to her shoulder. Liz could see that she was a heartbeat from pulling the trigger. With the sound of her father's whimpering in her ear, she started to edge round the table in the hope she could get close enough to rush her and deflect her aim.

Time, distance, fate's decree were all against her. The sound of a shotgun blast echoed around the walls like a thunderclap, burrowed its way into her brain, the shock turning her body as rigid as a soldier's at attention. Her eyes dragged themselves to her father. He was on his knees, staring up at his wife in horror. Blood was seeping through a hole in his chest, diffusing like a red army let off the leash, staining his white shirt. He transferred his gaze to the blood and then, with a look of disbelief, toppled onto the floor so that Liz lost sight of him.

She tried to move, couldn't, stood there dumbstruck, part of her disbelieving, telling herself this must be a nightmare from which she would soon awaken. The woman turned to face her, a naughty child's smirk playing on her lips that gave way to a lost, forlorn look. The shotgun rose in her hands for a second time. Liz could no longer restrain herself. The scream that burst from her lips was swallowed by another shotgun blast.

★　★　★

Halted yards from the gate, Alex was turning to his younger colleague to give him last-minute instructions when the shotgun went off. Their eyes met for a moment as though both needed reassurance their ears had not deceived them. From the slightly stunned look that entered the DC's eyes, Alex discerned he understood that, in the blink of an eye, what had been looking like a straightforward arrest had more than likely changed to something else, possibly fraught with danger. But there was no time for advice now and he led the way, opening the gate and sprinting up the path, dreading what he might find inside the cottage because he was the one responsible for the outcome of the operation and right now the weight of it was heavy on his shoulders.

Halfway up the path, a second blast echoed into the night. Alex halted momentarily and, with an audible exhalation, the DC crashed into him. As they disentangled, Alex heard a screech, which he thought was a human scream until an owl launched itself from the cottage eaves, passing so close he heard the swoosh of its wings and felt the eerie touch of talons brushing his hair. He shivered involuntarily, started down the path again

249

and, finding the door unlocked, warned himself to be wary as he stepped inside, half expecting at any second to hear a third blast of the shotgun, this time meant for him.

When he entered the kitchen, all he could hear was the kitchen clock, which seemed to be keeping time with the thumping of his heart. Everything appeared perfectly normal until he advanced and was confronted with a scene that, in spite of his experience, horrified him. The colonel was lying in a pool of blood between the table and the sink unit. On the floor, not far from where he lay, he could see a pair of women's legs, the rest of her hidden by the table. Acid rose from his stomach, brought a bitter taste to his mouth. Surely it could only be Liz Hunt lying there! He tried to move himself but his limbs wouldn't obey until he became aware of the DC hovering at his shoulder. That jolted him out of his paralysis and he started forward, each step an effort as though his own reluctance to face the truth was creating an invisible force field between him and the woman.

He closed his eyes, preparing himself. When he opened them again and looked down there was a moment of guilty elation because it wasn't Liz Hunt. The woman lying there with a gaping hole in her chest was much older and her face was set in a smile as though she'd purged herself of whatever demons had pursued her in this world and had met death as a welcome release. A shotgun lay next to her body. Alex was a little ashamed to admit to himself that he was relieved it wasn't Liz Hunt, though with the smell of death in the air there was no cause for celebration and, anyway, where was Liz Hunt?

'This one's still breathing, sir!'

Alex turned to the DC, who was bending over the colonel's body, holding a towel against the hole the shotgun had blown in his chest. His phone was in his other hand and he seemed to be well in control of his emotions.

'Get emergency services out here!' Alex said. 'And armed response.'

A worrying thought struck him. Had Liz Hunt shot her father and the mystery woman then made her escape? Had she been intending to take revenge on her father all along and simply used him to do so? He dreaded the thought because it would mean his judgment of her had been badly flawed, the risk he'd taken naïve and foolhardy.

A soft whimpering sound reached his ears. It was coming through a half-open door at the far end of the kitchen. Dog or human, he couldn't tell which as he drew in a deep breath and stole through the doorway to find himself in darkness. He felt for the switch, found it and, when the light came on, was standing in a room that reeked of money, from the huge state-of-the-art television screen mounted on one wall to the miniature bar in the corner. An ornate chandelier added a real touch of class. Yet the room seemed cold and functional, as though it were a display set in a furniture store meant to be admired, rather than a lived-in home. He didn't dwell on the ambience, however, because his eyes were drawn to the figure in the corner sitting in a low rocking chair, the only piece of furniture of any antiquity. To his great relief, it was Liz Hunt, tears streaming down her cheeks as she rocked back and forth like someone demented.

He went towards her, worrying about her mental state, especially when she showed no sign she was aware of his presence and continued her rocking motion, as though the quicker she moved the more she was able to distance herself from whatever had happened in the kitchen. Alex reached out, placed his hand on her shoulder.

'It's over, Liz,' he said. 'All over.'

It seemed to break the spell. Her rocking slowed and she looked up.

'This was my mother's chair,' she said, her

voice forlorn. 'It's all that's left of her.'

He guessed that she'd retreated to the past for comfort, to memories of her mother as a means to escape the threat the present posed to her sanity. He decided this wasn't the moment to winkle out of her what had happened, not when she appeared to be in such a delicate state of mind. There'd be time for that later. He just hoped she hadn't flipped, used the shotgun. Bad enough it had all gone awry without that.

'Danny will be worrying about you,' he said, cajolingly, hoping that mentioning her husband's name would be reassuring. 'Let's go and see him, shall we?'

It did the trick because she brightened up, rose willingly and took Alex's arm. To avoid the bloodfest in the kitchen, he led her to the front door, exited that way. Two armed policemen spotted them as they came round the side of the building into the back garden. Recognizing the DI, they moved off the path so they could pass. Their sirens' ululations in grating discord, two ambulances were already speeding up the lane firing splinters of blue light into the darkness. Alex heard someone calling him and turned to see the DC approaching. He looked wary and bemused.

'What do you want me to do, sir?' he asked. 'Are you coming back inside to take over?'

Alex disabused him of that notion. 'No, I'm going to the hospital with this lady. This is your chance to show your capabilities so go back in there and show what you can do.'

He knew as senior officer it was wrong of him to leave the scene of the crime but he was so worried about Liz Hunt, felt so responsible for her plight, that he wanted to make sure she was in the right hands as soon as possible. When the ambulances parked in the road and the paramedics stepped through the gate, he told them what had happened and stayed by her side as they led her to the ambulance, then climbed inside himself.

As the doors closed, it felt like the final curtain coming down in a tragic play. But Alex knew the crucial difference was that there would be no calm, measured reflection on tonight's action for Liz Hunt, because the repercussions would never really end for her. She was sitting opposite him draped in a blanket and he was relieved to see a change for the better seemed to have occurred in her mental state. No longer sobbing, she was meeting Alex's gaze as though she had something to say to him.

'Want to talk, or rather not just now?' he inquired tentatively, half hoping she'd reply in the negative because he was afraid when she opened up it might be to confess she was the one who'd used the shotgun.

She nodded and, hardly faltering, poured it all out. Alex would never have guessed at Robert Walker's pedigree, nor that the colonel would have gone so far to hide it. The colonel's second wife, Janet, whom Liz had never seen before, must have gone off her head. After she'd shot the colonel, she'd turned the shotgun on Liz, who had feared for her life. But then, as though it was a pleasure to end her misery, she'd put the barrel against her own chest and pulled the trigger. At that point, her nerves stretched to breaking point, Liz had run out of the room.

Alex could see it clearly now, old sins echoing down the years, suppressed emotions bubbling away, only needing a spark to set them off. Liz had been an innocent bystander and, although that was a relief, he was angry at himself because he'd put her in such danger after promising she'd be protected. In his defence, nobody could possibly have foreseen the denouement. Hopefully, Liz would see that and find it in her heart to forgive him.

'I'm so sorry,' he mumbled. 'Shouldn't have been so sure — '

She shook her head. 'Not your fault. My father was the one to blame and he got what he deserved. Nobody deserves to die like that, I know . . . but neither did Robert Walker or my husband's friends.' A single tear dropped from her eye. 'I wish I could have had a proper father.'

'He's not dead yet, Liz. He might make it, though I doubt it.'

She was silent for a moment. 'Better he does die. What use is he? What use has he ever been?'

They said very little for the rest of the journey. When they arrived at the hospital, he made sure she was in the right hands then took a taxi back to headquarters, picked up his own car and headed straight back to the cottage. Hopefully, his young colleague had coped in his absence, hadn't made any blunders, otherwise he'd be in big trouble for deserting the crime scene and leaving him in charge.

★   ★   ★

Two weeks after that horrific night Alex was at his desk, a tedious pile of paperwork in front of him. The colonel's case had proved to be clear cut and he'd received praise for his initiative, particularly his prompt action on the moors. What pleased him most was that Robert Walker had received justice. His killer was in hospital, hanging on to life. Even if he survived, he had nothing to look forward to other than life in prison. His daughter, who'd recovered from the horror of that night at the cottage, had declared she had no intention of ever seeing him again. Alex couldn't blame her. She owed him no filial duty after what he'd done to her and to others.

His thoughts turned to his son, the difference it would have made to his own life if he was still here. Because of their ages, the geographical proximity of their deaths, most of all the wasted potential of two young lives, Jamie and Robert had become linked in his mind as though, beyond the grave, they had found an empathy and were calling out to him to find them justice. That was why he'd been so driven to find the soldier's killer. He supposed, subconsciously, he'd hoped solving the Walker case would act as a catharsis for his ongoing failure to find his son's murderer. Now he knew there was no chance of that happening. How could he ever have imagined it would make a difference? His failure to find who had killed Jamie would always plague him, and yet he knew there had been a subtle change in his attitude because he thought it unlikely now, after the passage of five years, that he would ever succeed. He needed to accept that or he would waste his own life, and he knew that would have been abhorrent to his son.

A knock on the door brought him out of his

reverie. When he called out, Liz Hunt entered, her husband a step behind. Smartly dressed and well groomed, they presented a different picture from the last time he'd seen them. Most pleasing was that the strained and hunted look was entirely gone. Alex thought they looked like a newly married couple.

He ushered them in and arranged two chairs, wondering what was behind the visit. Perhaps they'd thought of something relevant to the case, though he was pretty sure everything had been raked over with a fine-tooth comb.

'Well,' he said, smiling. 'Hope you're not here to report a crime.'

Both smiled shyly, looked from one to the other as though, now they were in his inner lair, they were not too sure of themselves. They appeared a little reticent, he thought, and hoped their terrible experiences hadn't knocked their spirits too much because it was their stubborn courage that had got them through. Danny nodded at his wife and she spoke first.

'We've come because we haven't had the chance to thank you properly,' she said, suddenly coming to the verge of tears. 'Not many would have taken the chance to help us and risk their own career in the process.'

Alex, embarrassed, wafted a hand. 'I have

no conscience about it because I know neither of you intended harm.' His eyes flitted to Danny. 'You never really thought your pals would go ahead with their scheme, did you?'

Danny shook his head. 'I thought they would see sense and forget it. It's still hard for me to believe. They were good men. Maybe if we hadn't gone to Afghanistan things . . . '

His voice trailed away and Liz grasped his hand. Alex thought he was a lucky man, Danny Hunt. He had a good wife, whose strength and loyalty had been proven under fire, metaphorically and literally. Without her, Afghanistan might have had another victim.

Alex leaned forward. 'For what it's worth my advice to you both is to put all that's happened right behind you. Close the book. Not easy, I know, but you've a lot of years ahead of you.'

'We'll try,' Danny told him. 'You've risked your career for us so we have to make something of our lives.'

Before Alex could say anything, Liz added, 'Danny told me you had a son who would be about his age if he hadn't been killed. I was so sorry.'

Innocently, she'd stepped into the badlands. Normally, he avoided talking about Jamie, what had happened, but this time, perhaps because it had been on his mind only moments ago, he found himself opening up.

'It was a dark night,' he said, transporting himself back in time. 'My son was at a party, a house not far from where Robert Walker died. He decided to take a stroll and was knocked down and killed.' Alex couldn't help himself, grimaced in disgust. 'The driver just left him there to die alone.'

He sighed, wishing now he hadn't told her. It never did any good, especially after the years that had passed. It elicited instant sympathy from most people but that was a wasted commodity which, however well meaning, made no difference in the end. Nothing did: not then, not now, not ever.

'I'm so sorry,' Liz said again and the inevitable silence ensued.

'It happened on the first of August, five years ago,' he mumbled just for something to say. 'As you will understand, the date is etched in my mind forever.'

He noticed the colour draining from Liz's face, as though he'd just announced a death.

'First of August, five years ago.'

Her voice was a lugubrious drone. She was staring at Alex but he could tell something else, something deep in her memory, was competing for her attention at that moment and winning hands down.

Perplexed, he simply nodded and she

260

shivered as though an unseen presence in the room had suddenly laid a freezing hand on her shoulder. Eyelids fluttering, like someone emerging from a dream world, not sure of her surroundings and needing reassurance, she turned to her husband.

'What is it?' Danny said, putting a hand on her shoulder.

'That was the day I left home . . . came to you.' She slid her eyes back to Alex, clearly in a state of agitation. 'That date is burned in my memory, too.'

Alex waited, wondering what was coming next. She'd intimated the date was somehow significant in her life but surely that was only coincidence at play and coincidence shouldn't be causing her such obvious anxiety. He began to wonder whether, despite outward appearances, her experience in that cottage was working away under the surface, affecting her nervous system and allowing her imagination to stray beyond reasonable bounds.

Danny put his arm right around her. 'What's upsetting you so much, love?'

She stared at the floor and muttered, 'There's more and it's hard to say it, Danny, but I have to.'

Alex waited silently, wondering what was coming. When, eventually, she lifted her head, he noticed the vagueness was gone from her eyes, a spark of determination in its place. Tilting her jaw, she looked him in the eye.

'I need to tell you something, Inspector. It might turn out to be meaningless but you need to know. It's the least I can do.'

Alex frowned. 'Fire away, then, and we'll decide whether it's meaningless or not.'

He leaned back and listened while she recounted what had happened the night she'd run away from home never to return again. As the tale unfolded, Alex sat further forward and concentrated on her every word. When she'd finished, he was staggered, wondered whether, after years of unanswered prayer, providence was at last leaning towards his side.

★　★　★

The uniform on duty outside the colonel's private ward recognized Alex immediately and gave him the nod to go straight in. He knew the guard was probably wondering why he was there because the man inside was seriously ill, was simply lingering now. He would probably never stand trial so why bother a man who would soon die?

In truth, this was the last place Alex expected to find himself. Liz Hunt made it crystal clear she didn't want to see her father, felt no filial love or loyalty, only a deep loathing for him and his crimes. The colonel, on his part, hadn't asked to see her and had shown no remorse. It was going to be difficult enough to overcome his own deep loathing of a man who could batter his own flesh and blood to death but there was a personal matter he had to clear up, questions which, if they remained unanswered, would haunt him for the rest of his life. He only hoped, if his suspicions were confirmed, he would be able to control himself.

He felt his breathing accelerate and hesitated a moment before he entered. Telling himself not to raise his expectations too high, because, after all was said and done, he could be on a wild goose chase and, when he stepped outside again, might be none the wiser, he took in a deep breath, reminded himself the soldier might not be in a fit enough state to answer or, in keeping with a twisted nature, might refuse to do so. If that was the case, Alex hoped he'd be able to cope with the disappointment of having to return to that state of limbo with which he'd been cursed for so long.

White curtains hid the patient's bed. Over in the corner, a middle-aged nurse busied herself at a washbasin. She sensed him standing there, turned, shot him a querulous look that was close to outright anger. Her tone of voice did its best to match the severity of her stare.

'Can't you let him rest, the state he's in?'

Alex wanted to tell her about the colonel's victims, the trail of destruction he'd left in his wake but managed to restrain himself.

'I've one last question for him,' he said wearily, 'and it's important.'

Frowning her disapproval, and with a scathing glance that must have withered many a junior nurse, she walked past him to the door, called out as she exited.

'Ten minutes maximum!'

Alex didn't waste time, opened the curtains and stood beside the bed. The colonel was lying flat, besieged by machines and tubes, modern technology helping him fight what was likely to be his last battle.

He pulled up a chair and sat down. The soldier's eyes were closed and he wondered whether his visit was going to be futile, especially when he called his name without eliciting any response. He reached out intending to touch his shoulder but before he could complete the action the colonel, seeming to sense his presence, opened his eyes and slowly swivelled his head so that he was looking directly at him. It was obvious he was in pain but Alex felt not a morsel of sympathy for him.

'Get out of here,' the colonel groaned. 'Give me peace, for God's sake!'

Alex narrowed his eyes 'For God's sake, is it? That's rich coming from a man like you. You dare to invoke God's name after all your sins?'

He hadn't decided on any tactics he would use to approach the matter that brought him to the colonel's bedside, had made up his mind to play it by ear, follow instincts, which had served him well in his work up to now.

'Soldiers turn to God in the carnage of battle,' the colonel answered, his voice straining. 'Who knows whether they're deluded or not? I'll probably find out soon enough.'

'Open mind, then?'

A spasm of pain jolted the colonel's body making him grimace. Alex wondered whether he was going to lose him before he had answered the question he'd come here to ask. But the spasm passed and he settled again.

'Open mind, you say? Never thought about it . . . much. Too busy . . . getting on. Too late now for all that.'

'Maybe,' Alex said, fixing his eyes on the colonel, trying to infuse his gaze with meaning, 'you should have thought more about it when you had the chance.'

The soldier averted his eyes, stared up at the ceiling. 'Too many sins,' he muttered, more to himself than Alex. 'Too far down the path to suddenly become humble.'

Alex sensed this was a vital moment. It was the first time the colonel had shown the faintest sign of remorse. Lying there in pain, with nothing more to do than think about his past, the meaning of his life and what might lie in store for him, had probably stirred his withered conscience. Perhaps, in that frame of mind, he'd be willing to talk about other past misdemeanours.

'There's something I need from you,' Alex said. 'It might bring us both a measure of peace.'

Alex was surprised how controlled his voice sounded. It didn't reflect the nervous tension, which had been building up inside him since Liz Hunt had spoken to him that morning. Right now his intestines felt as though a mad musician was plucking away at them with a plectrum.

The colonel didn't look at him and he thought he was deliberately blanking him out of sheer obduracy, had no intention to co-operating. But suddenly, just when he was beginning to lose hope, he turned his gaze back to him and Alex saw a flicker of the old arrogance.

'Why should I give you anything — a man who brought me to this?'

Alex felt like reaching out and strangling

him but managed to maintain his calm façade. Affecting what he hoped looked like a nonchalance he wasn't feeling, he shrugged his shoulders.

'Because, for you, nothing matters now. Because if you're called to answer . . . afterwards . . . ' Alex paused. He'd used all his ammunition up in one blast and was struggling to amass any more weaponry.

'You sound like a priest,' the colonel moaned, 'and that won't wash with me. If I needed a priest I'd — '

A gurgling noise ascended his throat, drowned the sentence. But Alex had already caught his drift, had expected no more, really, from a man like him. Now his only recourse was to come right to the point, hope against hope he might relent.

'No priest,' he said. 'Just a grieving father who wants to know who killed his son so he can have some peace.'

The soldier frowned. 'I've no idea what you're talking about.'

'Then hear me out and tell me the truth. The truth is all I want.'

The soldier listened as Alex repeated Liz's story of how one dark night, five years ago, he'd returned to the cottage with blood on his clothes, saying he'd knocked a sheep over and lifted it off the road. He'd put the soiled clothes straight in the washing machine, hosed down his car then hit the whisky bottle, growing more abusive towards his daughter with each glass he downed, blaming her for all that was wrong in his world. For her, it was the final straw. She'd walked out with nothing but the clothes she stood in and never returned.

The colonel didn't interrupt and his face remained impassive. When he'd finished speaking, the detective sighed, looked him in the eye and laid all his cards on the table.

'My son was killed that same night, no more than a few miles from your cottage . . . a hit-and-run driver. For five years I've been tormented — not knowing. Now, I'm left wondering whether it really was a sheep you knocked down or . . . my son, God rest his soul.' Alex lowered his voice to almost a whisper. 'I'm hoping now that you've got nothing to lose there's enough humanity left in you to enlighten me one way or another.'

Alex hated asking anything from this man, didn't think he'd be capable of much contrition for past acts but he'd had to try. A minute passed, the colonel looking straight ahead, his face pale, immobile and emotionless, as though it were a mere verisimilitude of a human face carved from a piece of white marble and lacking a vital spark that made it human. Alex thought he was shutting him out, his chance of finding the truth gone. But then the soldier rallied, ran his tongue round his lips and, still not looking at the detective, spoke in a monotone.

'I'd had too much to drink. It was a dark night. I didn't see the lad. It was an accident.'

Alex always believed, if he ever found the person who had killed his Jamie, he'd tear him apart on the spot, but instead he felt entombed in ice, numb from head to toe, not fired with the heat of his fury as he'd expected to be. He stared at his son's killer, at those bloodless lips from which, after all this time, the truth had emerged, and knew he couldn't take revenge on a creature already hovering between this world and the next, whose own deviant actions had led to his nemesis. He understood, then, that it was finally over. Though its path had been circuitous, justice had descended upon the colonel for Jamie's death, indeed for all his crimes, and he would no longer have to feel he'd failed his son.

'Tell me,' he said, 'did getting away with it give you the confidence to think you could kill Robert Walker and hire those hit men without being caught?'

The colonel pursed his lips and Alex thought he detected a flash of the old arrogance, a will that would not be deflected if he wanted something. Ultimately, like a spoiled child who knows no constraints, thinking he was above the law he'd reached too far.

'I'd have managed it if it wasn't for my daughter, if I hadn't nurtured a viper in my bosom.'

Alex shook his head in disgust. 'No, you wouldn't. There's always one more temptation for your kind. What goes around comes around. It just takes time is all.'

There didn't seem any more to say, nor any point in lingering. It was best to walk away, leave the colonel to die, plagued, he hoped, by what remained of his conscience and not mourned by anyone. He rose, took one last look at the man who had torn his life apart, turned his back and walked to the door.

As he stepped out of the ward, that numb feeling returned. His legs seemed to move by sheer force of habit rather that of his own volition and the sharp, staccato snap of his shoes echoing on the floor was like muted gunfire from miles away. Gradually, the feeling dissipated and he was back in the world again. He didn't suppose for one minute discovering the truth was going to make him happier because it couldn't bring his son back. But at least it was no longer a mystery who had killed his son. It was just a pity he hadn't found that out years ago, before the colonel wreaked havoc in other lives.

★ ★ ★

As Alex drove through rush hour traffic, the day was beginning to fade, purple striations lying on the horizon like vast mountain ranges redolent of mysteries beyond the ken of this world. He suddenly felt strangely alone, his car a metal cocoon shutting him off temporarily from that world outside which was indifferent to his existence, to problems that were of no significance except to him. He studied the faces of his fellow commuters, wondered whether any of them were experiencing a similar feeling of isolation, guessed not. Most, he imagined, would be hurrying home to their families while, since Jamie's premature demise, he'd had no one to go home to, only the demands of the job to occupy his life. He knew perfectly well that what had brought about his melancholy line of thought was learning about Jamie's death. The quest to find out had been driving him and, now that need had been satisfied, floodgates were already opening to other feelings, which he'd been denying. For sure, in this mood he didn't feel like going back to his flat, so instead he headed for headquarters, ended up in his office half an hour later grateful there weren't many people around because he didn't fancy exchanging pleasantries or office badinage tonight.

He switched on the desk lamp, sat in semi-gloom in a reflective mood, struck by a paradox; nothing had changed, really, yet everything had changed. He'd still go on working in these familiar surroundings but today marked the end of a chapter in his life and, like it or not, a new page would take him in a different direction. Like a long-term prisoner newly released into a changed world, he felt a little frightened, not least of himself. How would he cope?

The thought had barely passed through his mind when there was a rap on the door. When he called out, rather tetchily, his visitor entered, stood in the shadow beyond the curve of light cast by the desk lamp. He could make out a woman's shape, but it took him a moment to realize it was Sandra Best standing there. He gestured rather clumsily towards the chair and she stepped into the full glare of the light, sat down, crossed her legs and stared at him with an expression he found hard to interpret.

'How did it go?' she asked.

He didn't know what she was talking about. Had he missed something?

'How did what go, Sandra?'

'Your trip to the hospital.'

Alex was confused. How did she know he'd gone there? He hadn't told anybody, didn't want anybody to know.

She saw his confusion and quickly elaborated.

'Liz Hunt came to see me, told me you were going to visit her father and the reason why. She said she was very worried about you, thought you might need company after you'd seen him.'

'She shouldn't have told you anything about that!'

'Come on,' Sandra said, raising an eyebrow. 'The girl was only thinking of your feelings. Thoughtful of her, if you ask me.'

Though disgruntled, he knew she was right, that Liz Hunt had only been trying to be kind. Her woman's intuition must have told her that Sandra could be trusted and coincidentally, the one person in the world whose company he thought he could stand at this moment, was sitting right there in front of him.

When he was slow to speak Sandra looked embarrassed and made to rise.

'As long as you're all right, I'll just go.

Don't want to pry.'

Making a motion with his hand to indicate he wanted her to stay, he said, 'The colonel confessed he did it. He ran down Jamie in his car and killed him.'

He wondered how he could speak those words, so stark and pitiless-sounding, as though Jamie was just another statistic on the murder roll. A tear started to form in the corner of his eye and he leaned back into the shadows so Sandra wouldn't see his face.

'Are you going to be okay?' Sandra inquired.

He swallowed hard. 'I needed to find who was responsible for Jamie's death. At least I know now.'

'So how do you feel?'

'I feel . . . I don't know . . . satisfied in a way, but empty . . . like something inside me has gone away and left a void.'

There was a small silence and she leaned forward into the light. He noticed it added an extra sheen to her lustrous red hair. Her blue eyes assessed him, not in a cold, distant way, the way he'd seen her with criminals, but softly, with what he thought was a deep concern. More than ever, he was aware of what he'd lost when he'd pushed her away.

'You're bound to feel that way but you'll come through it, if not for yourself for Jamie's sake. Jamie wasn't selfish. He loved you and he would want you to be happy.'

Alex cleared his throat. 'That's the one thing I'm certain of but it doesn't make it any easier.'

Sandra dropped her eyes for a moment, then suddenly snapped them back at him, their intensity drawing him in.

'It might not be any consolation and maybe I shouldn't say it, but I'm . . . proud of you.'

Alex felt himself blush, was glad he was in the shadows so she couldn't see. He had no idea what she meant, could only hazard a guess.

'I didn't do anything,' he stuttered. 'Liz took all the risks to get her father to confess.'

She narrowed her eyes wickedly. 'Not at all what I meant. You gave those young people a second chance when their lives could have been ruined. Took a risk with your own career to do it, didn't . . . play by the book. That was really something.'

Now he really was embarrassed. It wasn't just what she'd said, it was the way she was looking at him now, that same tenderness there he remembered from when they were together all those years ago. He was confused, not sure what was going on, afraid he would misinterpret that look, make himself appear foolish, so he didn't dare speak. Yet, ultimately, the words refused to be corralled, slipped from his lips without him thinking about them, as though they'd been there waiting without his knowing.

'I could do with a second chance myself.'

Sandra leaned back into the shadows so he couldn't see the expression on her face but he was sure he must have embarrassed her. He cursed himself for his outburst. What had he been thinking?

Her voice came to him from beyond the light.

'I always thought Lauren Bacall got it wrong when she told Bogart, 'All you've got to do is whistle'.'

'How so?' he mumbled, his throat desiccated. Was this going to be the biggest put-down of all time? If so, he figured he probably deserved it.

'Whistling is strictly for calling canines. Far better if she'd said, 'All you've got to do is ask me'. Much less subservient.'

It was a rather obscure response but Alex thought it sounded more encouraging than otherwise. Hoping he wasn't misreading her entirely, he decided, having gone this far, he might as well drive right off the cliff.

'I ain't Bogie and I never could whistle.' He took a deep breath. 'But I'm asking if you'll give me a second chance, Sandra Best

. . . even though I know I don't deserve one.'

She didn't answer straight away and he convinced himself she was trying to find a way to let him down gently. Then, as he held his breath, she brushed back a loose strand of hair and spoke.

'First, I have to tell you why I came back.'

With a quizzical expression, he said, 'You don't have to. What difference could it make?'

She leaned into the full glare of the light, smiled at him in a strange, enigmatic way.

'I'd prefer it if you knew. You see, I came back to Teesside because I liked the area but also because I thought you and I had . . . unfinished business. I actually asked to be assigned to your team. DCI Smithers, bless him, agreed not to tell you that.'

Alex was amazed. It never crossed his mind that their working together had been any more than a vagary of fate. Now that he thought about it, Smithers had behaved strangely towards him. No wonder, when he'd been playing Cupid's little helper — an eminent piece of miscasting.

'Time had passed,' she continued. 'I wasn't sure whether you had changed, withdrawn further into yourself. Doing what you did for that young couple convinced me you were the same man I fell for. So, yes, I would like to try again.'

Alex's face lit up. In the space of a few hours, he had learned who had killed his son and that Sandra was prepared to give him another chance. Days like this didn't come along very often in life. Today was a new beginning but one he could feel optimistic about.

'Thank God for that,' he said, then instantly turned sombre. 'I'm sorry I pushed you away before. I really am.'

She held her hand up to stop him saying more. 'No apologies, or regrets, just a clean start and we'll see where it takes us.'

'Can't say fairer than that,' Alex said and winked. 'Now let's get out of here. There's more to life than work . . . or so they tell me.'

We do hope that you have enjoyed reading this large print book.

Did you know that all of our titles are available for purchase?

We publish a wide range of high quality large print books including:
Romances, Mysteries, Classics
General Fiction
Non Fiction and Westerns

Special interest titles available in large print are:
The Little Oxford Dictionary
Music Book
Song Book
Hymn Book
Service Book

Also available from us courtesy of Oxford University Press:
Young Readers' Dictionary
(large print edition)
Young Readers' Thesaurus
(large print edition)

For further information or a free brochure, please contact us at:
Ulverscroft Large Print Books Ltd.,
The Green, Bradgate Road, Anstey,
Leicester, LE7 7FU, England.
Tel: (00 44) 0116 236 4325
Fax: (00 44) 0116 234 0205

Other titles published by Ulverscroft:

STONE COLD

Peter Taylor

Former gypsy prize-fighter, Henry Torrance, is about to be released from prison where he's been serving time for killing fellow bare-knuckle fighter Bull Jackson. Now, he's resolved to get his life on track and settle down with his girlfriend Mary. However, the criminal Jackson family is insistent that Henry should fight their latest protege and Henry's brother and father accept the challenge on his behalf. As the day of the big fight draws closer, Henry's determination not to return to his old ways is countered by the mounting pressure on him. Can he ever escape his dark past?